1
F
MURDER

DIG
FOR
MURDER

Roger Keevil

a Ramston murder mystery

also by Roger Keevil

THE INSPECTOR CONSTABLE MURDER
MYSTERIES
Murderer's Fête
Murder Unearthed
Death Sails In The Sunset
Murder Comes To Call
Murder Most Frequent
The Odds On Murder
No Bar To Murder
The Murder Cabinet
The Game Of Murder

THE COPPER & CO MURDER MYSTERIES
Honeymooner's Murder
Murder At Witch's Holt
Buccaneer's Murder

THE RAMSTON MURDER MYSTERIES
Murdered By Moonlight
Manuscript For Murder
The Whodunnit Murder

DIG FOR MURDER

by

Roger Keevil

Cover design by Christopher Brooke

Copyright © 2024 Roger Keevil

The moral right of the author has been asserted.

'Dig For Murder' is a work of fiction and wholly the product of the imagination of the author. All persons, events, locations, organisations, establishments and alpacas are entirely fictitious or are used fictitiously, and are not intended to resemble in any way any actual persons or alpacas living or dead, events, locations, organisations, or establishments. Any such resemblance is entirely coincidental, and is wholly in the mind of the reader.

Chapter 1

"Ron!"

The urgency in his wife's voice brought Ron Faye out of the kitchen and into the sitting room at a run, potato-peeler still clutched in his hand, to find Tania transfixed by the television screen, where a rain-coated reporter was speaking into a microphone in front of a farm gate.

"What's up, love?"

"Shhh!"

"*... and while so far the police have been reluctant to release details, we understand that the dead man has now been unofficially identified as a Professor Malcolm Sutherland, the leader of the archaeological team who have been carrying out excavations at the site of the Upson Downs long barrow. Other than saying that the death is regarded as suspicious, the Wessex Constabulary are remaining tight-lipped. As are the local alpacas.*" A smirk. "*And now, back to the studio.*"

"*Thank you, Oliver. And now, the weather ...*"

Tania switched off the sound and turned to her husband, a look of concern on her face. "That's what Dennis Dean was telling us about this lunchtime at the Cross Keys, isn't it?"

"Yes," replied Ron with a smile. "And don't I remember you saying that you'd had quite enough of murders, and that three were plenty to be going on with, thank you very much? In fact, I seem to recall you repeating a very famous quote from a certain prime minister – 'No, no, no!'"

"Yes, but ..."

"Mind you," conceded Ron, "funny that the dead chap's name is Sutherland. I wonder if he's any relation to Leah."

Tania let out a gusty sigh of annoyance. "Honestly, Ron, sometimes I wonder what you're using for brains. Wasn't Malcolm the name of one of the men Leah used to be married to? And I've got a vague recollection that she said he was an archaeologist. He must be her ex-husband."

Ron raised his eyebrows. "Wow! That's one hell of a coincidence."

"It's more than that," continued Tania. "Don't you remember that we all went up to Leah's place for the R.O.A.D.S. Summer Picnic a few years back? All the members of the dramatic society went along."

"How could I forget?" replied Ron ruefully. "That was the time that one of the Kents' kids sat on an ants' nest, and I got stung by a wasp. And while I was running about, one of the alpacas ate my cake."

"But didn't you see where that reporter was standing?" insisted Tania. "Don't you recognise that gateway? And he mentioned alpacas! It's the entrance to Leah's farm!"

*

'They can't close us down,' thought Edward Wilton, as he stood grim-faced watching the activity before him. 'They simply can't. This site is too important. If they try, I shall have something to say. I'm not without friends. And maybe this time they'll get their priorities right and put me in charge from the start.'

Edward had, at the age of fifty-two, achieved a milestone which many people in his position would regard as the pinnacle of their profession. And with his high forehead, thinning sandy hair and fussy toothbrush moustache, he looked every part the cliché academic. From the day when, playing mud-pies in the garden at seven years old, he had unearthed a Roman coin which turned out to be an extremely rare aureus from the reign of the Emperor Maxentius, he had developed a fascination for all things archaeological. From then on, his career had followed an almost predetermined path. Curator of his junior school's tiny museum, with its glass case of flint arrowheads, shepherd's crowns - fossilised sea-urchins discovered at the beach by fellow-pupils - and a fragment of a cuneiform mud-brick tablet from ancient Sumeria, he went on to study archaeology at university. He was never the most brilliant student, but his dogged determination earned him the quiet approval of his tutors. Indeed, on one occasion, during a field trip to Orkney, his refusal to abandon a part-excavated site which was under threat from a raging North Sea storm, with torrential rain and mountainous waves, had uncovered a vital piece of evidence which proved a crucial Viking origin, resulting in acclaim from the local authorities and a severe bout of pneumonia which had very nearly carried him off.

Even during student vacations, the lure of all things historical was impossible to resist. One holiday was spent as an experiences guide at the Jorvik museum in York. Another took him to the constantly-expanding site at Housesteads on Hadrian's Wall. The perfectly respectable degree which he earned on graduation led on to a period as an intern at the British Museum, during which he began to specialise in British history of the Bronze Age and the early medieval period. Employment at other museums followed, and he was even seen on a couple of occasions on television programmes about the history of Britain, offering an opinion on a fragment of pottery or the significance of traces of an ancient boundary ditch. And now he had achieved what most would regard as the crowning moment in his career – after only a year in the Department of Archaeology at the University of Camford, he had been appointed as the department's head, following his predecessor's sudden death from heat-stroke during a visit to a site in the Egyptian desert. The only fly in the ointment – the fact that the university authorities had felt that Edward was still too fresh in the post, and had seen fit to bring in an archaeologist from elsewhere to oversee the Upson

Downs dig.

'Perhaps it's an omen,' thought Edward, with a dark smile. 'One man dies, and I step in to replace him. And now, another. My chance, I think.'

*

'This is just what we need,' thought Mary Winterbourne, as she sat at her desk in the old Tack Room watching the reports on the BBC news website. 'They do say there's no such thing as bad publicity. I wonder,' she mused.

Attractive and in her late thirties, Mary oozed competence. An unexpected meeting in the bar tent at an agricultural fair had led to her being lured away from her former breathtakingly dull lettings job at a Westchester estate agency, whose failings she had laid out in expansive detail to her new acquaintance over several glasses of single malt. Because Leah Sutherland, her chance whisky-drinking companion, was at that very moment faced with the need to replace her previous site manager, who had on a sudden whim decided to abandon the UK for the rolling landscapes of New Zealand. A deal was struck, and Mary found herself in charge of the range of former agricultural buildings at Leah's farm, which now functioned as a set of holiday lets, having been converted when Leah abandoned all activities dairy and arable in favour of a new venture some years before. And with accommodation provided in the form of an apartment in the former piggery, Mary was very content to handle all matters involving both long-term visitors, cleaning and maintaining the holiday cottages, and those who came to the farm on day visits.

The phone on her desk rang, bringing her out of her reverie. "Good afternoon. Alpaca Max - Mary speaking ... Oh, hello, Mrs Ellis ... Yes, that's right. We've got your family booked in for tomorrow at ..." A swift glance at the wall chart in front of her. "... eleven o'clock ... Oh, I'm sorry to hear that. Why would that be? ...

Goodness! All three of them? ... Yes, it is unfortunate, isn't it? But children are so susceptible, aren't they? ... Yes, measles does seem to be doing the rounds at the moment ... Well, yes, I quite understand. And they were all so looking forward to the walk, weren't they? Of course, I'm afraid we won't be able to refund your deposit, but we'll gladly hold on to it and set it against a future visit. Would you have any idea when that might be? ... Oh. Very well. In that case, I'll wait to hear from you ... Yes. Thank you for letting me know. Good..." Mary was left holding a silent telephone receiver.

'And so it begins,' she thought, as she replaced the phone. 'And so much for bad publicity. I wonder how many more calls like that I shall be getting. Why on earth that wretched man had to ...' She suppressed the thought with a sigh, and swept a hand through her mop of light-brown hair. 'Oh well. I suppose I'd better go and tell Leah the good news.' She pushed back her chair, stood, and headed out of the Tack Room in the direction of the main farmhouse.

*

Victoria Whaddon lay back on the bed in her room in Tumulus Cottage and scrolled aimlessly through social media on her phone. 'This is terminally boring,' she thought. 'And just when things were starting to get interesting.'

Victoria, a twenty-two year old Masters student at Camford University, had jumped at the chance to volunteer to work on the Upson Downs dig when the opportunity was offered to her. Intending to specialise in osteo-archaeology, she felt it fitted in perfectly with the subject of her further studies. It had long been thought that the Edwardians had comprehensively exhausted the site when a local land-owner and keen amateur historian, Lord de la Mere, had conducted investigations in the early years of the twentieth century. Some bones were found, along with fragments of beakers and tiny elements of glass jewellery, with the prize discovery, an almost intact bronze dagger, donated amidst great pomp to the County Museum in Westchester. However, new documents had recently come to light in the county archives, which revealed that Sir James's expedition had only managed to investigate four out of the five barrows at the site. The fifth, less prominent than its fellows and slightly apart from the main grouping, had been left until last, but when the First World War broke out, activities were suspended. Sadly, the only son and heir of the de la Meres had become a casualty of the war, and when peace returned, his lordship had no heart to continue the work. A newly-discovered letter in the Wessex county archives had provoked fresh interest in the remaining barrow, and a decision was made that the Archaeology Department of the University of Camford would mount a dig at the Upson Downs site.

And so far, the results had exceeded all expectations. The barrow had proved far larger than anticipated, having apparently been constructed in a hollow which had over the passage of time been filled in by wind, weather, and agricultural activity. Excavations had revealed a stone-flanked doorway which led to a passage into the centre of the structure, and off this passage, partially-collapsed stone-lined chambers yielded some astonishing finds. To the left, the remains of a young man, perhaps a warrior, as evidenced by the shadow of a wooden shield placed upon the body and a bronze item of jewellery. And in the next chamber on the same side, a touching collection of bones indicated that a young woman and two tiny children had been placed together, with fragments of cloth apparently swathing them together. Were the three linked, and what tragedy might have led to their burial together? On the opposite side, the bones of an old woman were found in a crouched position surrounded by numerous glass and pottery beads, together with a bronze hand mirror, indicating that she was probably of considerable status. The second chamber on the right was empty of human remains, but did contain several earthenware pots holding as-yet-unidentified remnants of food. But the greatest excitement of all was reserved for the chamber at the end of the passage, seemingly the largest of the five, which it was hoped might reveal the body of a tribal chieftain. Work had only just begun in removing the earthen contents, when the discovery of the expedition's leader's dead body brought everything to a crashing halt.

'I don't see why the police can't just let me carry on with my work,' thought Victoria. 'All the bones are in the old hay-barn, well away from the barrow. Perhaps now I can actually get on with my work without any distractions.' She gave a dismissive snort and flicked her long blonde hair out of her eyes, before returning to her perusal of her phone screen.

*

Downstairs in Tumulus Cottage, Anne Langford switched off the television, with its rolling news coverage which was incessantly repeating the same stories with a total lack of fresh information, and made her way through to the kitchen. At least making a cup of tea would give her something to do.

Anne was somewhat of an unusual feature around the precincts of Camford University. Amidst the numerous youthful undergraduates, flocks of whom were constantly swirling around the town on fleets of bicycles, to the great peril of unwary pedestrians, she was one of the very few mature students. A widowed former primary school teacher in her early sixties, plump and grey-haired, she had reached an age when retirement seemed to offer many attractions, only to find that, with few friends and no immediate family, time hung heavy on her hands. She had never seemed to find the opportunity, or the inclination, to develop any hobbies, and an attempt to write a novel had petered out into inconsequentialities, once she had exhausted her modest fund of amusing anecdotes from her former young pupils. Then one day, browsing through the magazines in her local library in Westchester, an article caught her eye. It told of a woman very like herself who had found herself at a loose end, but who had been prompted to undertake a total change of direction by returning to education, but this time on the receiving end. The woman had enrolled on a university business studies course as a mature student, and was now working in the City of London as a financial consultant. And on the adjacent page of the magazine was an advertisement from Camford University, extolling their policy of inclusivity when it came to applications from would-be students. Inspired, Anne investigated further, and found that the History Department would happily offer her a place. And now, after an initial period of puzzled chuckling from her fellow course-members, Anne had been welcomed among their numbers, and in fact had become something of a mascot and mother-figure among her new friends. It caused both her and them considerable amusement whenever, socialising with them in the Students' Union, she was mistaken for one of the university dons.

The invitation which appeared on one of the college noticeboards, advertising for volunteers to take part in an archaeological dig, appealed to her, and she was accepted without difficulty. And to begin with, all seemed well, despite one or two problems. But now the greatest problem of all was the fact that, with this morning's discovery, the whole enterprise had screeched to a halt, and who knew what the next step would be?

The kettle boiled, and Anne poured the water into the pot. "Victoria!" she called up the stairs. "I've made some tea. Would you like a cup?"

*

The tiny hamlet of Upson Parva lay on the cusp of

two worlds, situated as it was on the edge of the lush woodland which filled the deep valley which sheltered its larger cousin Upson Major, some two miles below, just as the trees petered out, giving way to the softer outlines and huge skyscapes of the chalk downland which lent both communities its name. And in Woodbine, a picturesque cottage of flint and brick at the northernmost end of Upson Parva's straggle of houses, George Cheverell sat in an armchair, buried in thought.

It was interesting, he reflected, to see how the relationships of a disparate group of people, brought together under a string of unforeseen circumstances, developed. If that letter hadn't turned up in the county archives, nobody would have suspected that there was anything further to be found at the site of the Upson Downs barrows. If the Archaeology Department of the university hadn't got a sniff of it, there would have been no moves to initiate further investigations. If the head of the department hadn't been in post for such a brief period of time, there would probably have been no move to import a more distinguished academic from elsewhere to head the project. If there hadn't been a conveniently-sited set of holiday cottages immediately adjacent to the site, the group of people involved wouldn't have been thrown together into such close proximity, with all the potential for tensions which that afforded. And most fortunately of all, George mused with a smile of quiet satisfaction, the location of the site couldn't have been better placed, from his point of view.

George was an enthusiastic member of the Westchester Historical Society, whose monthly meetings ranged over subjects as varied as the continuing search for the lost final resting place of an Anglo-Saxon king, to the part the city played in the events of the English Civil War. Talks were given by guest speakers on all topics, from the clandestine preparations for D-Day which were devised beneath the roof of one of the county's grandest country houses under conditions of the utmost secrecy, to the scandalous revelations about the social lives of the Regency upper classes, as described in the diaries of a prominent female author. Pre-history was not neglected – the county's rich heritage included a forest of standing stones scattered across the landscape, several well-preserved hill forts, and a significant henge whose importance was only overshadowed by its larger and more famous brother some miles away. So when, at one meeting, the subject of the Upson Downs dig was mentioned, together with the fact that volunteers would be welcomed to assist, George was the first to put his name forward, and he was delighted to be invited to join the team. He was sure that, although in his late forties, his back and knees would cope. And he had been right - he had been closely involved in uncovering the string of finds which had emerged. The question now was, what would happen next?

*

Stephen Tisbury found himself gazing unfocussed at the screen of his laptop in his bedroom in Henge Cottage, before suddenly coming to and closing the lid with a gesture of despair. What was the point of trying to concentrate on course-work in the middle of this situation?

The History of Art course at Camford University was particularly suited to someone who had never been especially academically cerebral, or at home with matters mathematical or scientific, but who, when taken as a boy to his home town's art gallery on a school outing, had been fascinated by the array of works on display. From that day, he fell hopelessly in love with the worlds of Van Eyck and Van Dyck, of Giotto and Canaletto, of Monet and Modigliani. His teachers, surprised at the young Stephen's leanings amidst a class generally assumed destined to become either sharp-suited city boys in the world of business finance or, for the less quick-witted, what the academics referred to out of their hearing as 'spannermen', encouraged his studies to the extent that, when the time came to leave school, Stephen was the only one of his contemporaries to secure a place at Camford. The university embraced him, and he embraced the artistic feast spread before him.

Aged twenty, and in his second year, the boy Stephen was still very much visible in the young man. Tall, over six feet, and extremely thin, he seemed to have grown upwards without any accompanying filling-out. His face, with its strong bone structure and regular features, was unexpectedly handsome, and was topped by a youthful flop of bright ginger hair. There seemed to be a constant readiness to smile, but that smile was absent at the moment. He looked back over the events which had led to this moment. The notice on the board in the Students' Union regarding the forthcoming Upson Downs dig which had attracted the attention of the loose grouping of friends from the History of Art and Archaeology Departments - the chatter over who might take up the opportunity to participate - the overhearing of remarks from one particular person which had hardened his resolve to put his name forward - had led to the quiet satisfaction at having secured a place on the team. But what had started out with optimism had soon turned sour. Were opportunities irrevocably lost? He sighed. That all depended on how things turned out.

With a sudden burst of determination, he re-opened his laptop.

Chapter 2

"Leah!" Ron blinked with surprise at the figure standing on the doorstep. "What on earth are you doing here?"

"Looking for you," came the brusque reply in Leah Sutherland's no-nonsense Scots accent. "Or to be more exact, for your wife."

"Oh," was Ron's nonplussed response.

"Well? Are you going to invite me in, or what?"

"Of course." Ron stepped back and, as Leah forged her way towards the sitting room, called out, "We've got a visitor, love."

"Leah!" Tania, no less amazed than her husband, rose to her feet as their guest appeared. "This is a surprise. What can we do for you?"

"For a start, you can pour me a very large single malt," said Leah, settling herself into an armchair. Ron, swift on cue, opened the drinks cupboard and set about obeying orders. "And second, you can help sort out this pickle they've landed me with."

Leah Sutherland was a sturdy Scotswoman in her late fifties, of medium height, and with a bush of iron-grey hair swept back untidily. As a frequent director of the shows put on by the Ramston Operatic And Dramatic Society, the local theatrical group of which Tania and Ron were long-standing and prominent members, she was well-known to the pair, and had directed the production of 'A Midsummer Night's Dream' at an open-air theatre in Cornwall during which Tania's murder-solving skills had first been demonstrated. Her background was colourful, to say the least. In one of several former incarnations she had been a barrister, known around the courts as 'the attack dog', and there were tales that she had once worked on North Sea oil rigs, before disappearing in the direction of an opal mine in Australia. She had along the way acquired several husbands, although nobody dared ask exactly how many. Her present existence, however, seemed very normal by contrast. She owned a farm on the fringe of Upson Downs.

As Ron handed her her drink she took a deep draught and, with a sigh of relief, leaned back, stretched her legs with their lace-up biker boots out in front of her, and undid her trademark camouflage jacket to reveal dungarees over a lumberjack shirt. She pushed her horn-rimmed glasses up on to the top of her head and took a breath.

"You'll have heard, I take it?" she said.

There was little doubt as to what she meant. "The murder on your farm," responded Tania.

"It's not on my farm!" came the exasperated reply. "But that's what everybody's going to think, isn't it? Which is why we've had phone-call after phone-call all afternoon cancelling day visits and holiday bookings. And once the word gets around, you know what it's like. This is going to hammer my business. It's got to be sorted out."

"I've got a great idea," intervened Ron. "For a start, why don't I top up that drink of yours? And then you can tell us all about it. All we know is what we saw on the TV news."

"You've been to the farm, haven't you?" began Leah. "And I'm sure you know about the pre-historic site up on the Downs, Tania - just on the other side of my boundary fence," she added, with emphasis. "Not on my land at all. So, because somebody had unearthed some document or other with fresh information, Camford Uni decided they wanted to send an expedition to look into it. And because they found out that I have holiday cottages, they decided to rent some to house the people taking part. Oh, apart from one local chap from the village. All well and good - I was quite happy to have the income, and there was no reason why they should interfere with my business. So they turned up to start, and you could have knocked me down with a feather. Who do you think was in charge of the expedition? Malcolm!"

"Who was your ex-husband," clarified Tania.

"One of them," retorted Leah grimly. "Mister Charming, when I first met him. That was when I was working out of Aberdeen, and he was digging on some Pictish site nearby. Well, it didn't take long for the charm to wear off, so he had to go."

"Just a thought," interrupted Tania. "And I hope you don't mind me asking. Because as you say, you married again after Malcolm."

"Once or twice," agreed Leah with a grim chuckle.

"I was just wondering why you kept his name."

"Och, there's no mystery there, dear. Quite simply, I couldn't be bothered to change it. I was here and there all over the place, and what with the bother of getting new passports or altering things at the bank, the whole thing was too much faff. So I just stayed Sutherland. And Malcolm and I went our ways, and I haven't seen him in years. Imagine my surprise when he turned up on my doorstep with his merry band, all suntan and smiles, fresh from heading an expedition in Jordan. And a professor now, no less."

"What did you think of that?" wondered Tania.

"Not a great deal, to be honest," said Leah with a dry laugh. "But there's a lot of water gone under both our bridges since then, and we both chose to be perfectly civilised about the situation. I put him in The Bothy on his own, and the other people in a couple of the other cottages, and let them get on with it. And our paths have hardly crossed since. They got on with their dig, and I got on with my alpacas."

"That's something I've always meant to ask you about," said Ron. "I know you keep them, and we've even met a couple. Including the one who ate my cake," he muttered under his breath. "But I really have no idea how you make a living out of them. It's not like keeping cows or pigs or chickens, is it? You can't eat them. And you can't sell their eggs."

Despite the situation, Leah let out a merry chuckle. "It's perfectly simple, Ron. Wool and walkies."

"You what?" Ron frowned in puzzlement.

"You've heard of alpaca wool, Ron," insisted Tania with a hint of impatience. "Don't you remember that alpaca coat I saw once in Horrids? It was beautiful."

"I do," said Ron ruefully. "It also cost an arm and a leg."

"Premium product," smiled Leah. "There's a chap who comes to shear the animals every spring ..."

"Like sheep?"

"Exactly. But for a rather better price for the product. And away it goes to be processed into sweaters, coats and goodness-knows what."

"Fine. I get that. But walkies?"

"It's a growing trend, Ron. I'm surprised you don't know about it. In fact, the Kents came up with their boys last year for an alpaca walk. All our beasts are very friendly, so we put halters on them and off you all go for an hour's walk in the country, each with your own animal, down past the village and along through the river valley woods. It's very calming. You should try it."

"And people actually pay for this?" Ron was amazed.

"In increasing numbers," said Leah. She grimaced. "Until now, that is. Suddenly, after what happened this morning, nobody seems to want to come near."

"So what exactly did happen?" enquired Tania.

"They'd got on with their dig for over a week," said Leah. "And they weren't any trouble. They pretty much kept themselves to themselves, and I let them use the old hay-barn to lay out their finds and examine them. But then this morning, they had got together ready to start work, and there was no answer from Malcolm's cottage, so they came knocking at my door to see if he was in with me. Of course, I said no. And I called in on my manager Mary, but she said she hadn't seen him. Then somebody suggested that he might have gone on ahead to the site on his own, but somehow it didn't feel right, so we all went up to the barrow together. And when we got there, there he was, face down in the entrance to the main chamber, stabbed in the back."

"Dead?"

"As mutton," replied Leah shortly. "I checked. Stone cold. I made sure none of the others touched him. And it was obvious there was nothing to be done, so then I shepherded them all back down to the farm and got Mary to ring the police. Who turned up a while later."

"You must have been so shocked," observed Tania.

"You might say that," responded Leah drily.

"So what happened then?" asked Ron.

"Actually, the police inspector was very nice ..."

"Not like that Inspector Marion Bright last week," said Ron in an aside to Tania.

"No, this guy was very pleasant at first. Youngish chap - name of Copper."

"Ah," smiled Tania. "Inspector Copper, eh?"

"Must be back from his firearms course," put in Ron.

"Apparently," agreed Tania. "Our paths have crossed before, Leah. During the business at the abbey."

"Oh, so you know him? Well, that might be helpful."

"Hmmm. Not so sure. Not convinced he's my biggest fan." Tania raised a doubtful eyebrow. "But why do you say 'helpful'?"

"Because," explained Leah, "when I told him that I used to be married to Malcolm, there was something of a change in his attitude. I suppose it was because of the old cliché - you know, always look at the spouse first. Thank goodness I had a cast-iron alibi. I'd been down here at the theatre in Ramston helping to paint the set for next week's production with David Kent and the Talbots. And we didn't finish until gone 1.00a.m., so Martha Talbot suggested I could crash in their spare room. And to be honest, I was glad of the offer, because I was too knackered to face the drive back home. So I didn't get back until about half an hour before that knock on the door this morning."

"Lucky for you," observed Ron.

"Yes," said Leah, "but not so lucky for the others. If I didn't murder Malcolm, somebody else must have done. And the farm is sufficiently remote to rule out any random passing person. The road from Upson Parva goes to us and nowhere else. Besides, if anyone the alpacas aren't used to turned up in the middle of the night, they'd have made some sort of fuss. And everybody says they didn't hear a thing. The animals arc fine with strangers during the day, but they can get jumpy at night. The thing is, they're used to my staff and all the people involved with the dig. So I'm only left with one conclusion."

"And your fine analytical barrister's brain is telling you ..." enquired Tania.

"That it's one of the people at the farm. I'm hosting a murderer."

*

"So exactly what brings you to our door? Why was it that you wanted to speak to Tania?" asked Ron, although he had a ghastly feeling that he knew what the answer would be.

"You've an instinct, dearie," replied Leah simply, gazing at her friend in appeal. "You've a knack for working things out, things that don't even occur to the police. You can talk to people, whereas folks have a tendency to clam up when questioned by the boys in blue. You've proved that - what is it, twice now?"

"Three, actually, and the last time only a matter of hours ago," stated Ron. "Don't you think Tania needs a break from all that?"

Leah took a deep breath "Well, there's my thought, Ron," she replied. "Tania does need a break away from it all. Away from work, that is. So what better than for her to enjoy a little holiday in the countryside, where she can take advantage of the calming therapeutic effect of going for a few strolls with some friendly alpacas? As it happens, I've got a couple of holiday cottages going begging at the moment. So why don't the pair of you come and stay at the farm for a few days? You never know, you might come across something that could solve the case."

"You've thought this all through, haven't you?" said Tania with a grudging smile.

"It is quite a long drive from my place to yours," said Leah with an answering grin.

"But I don't see how this is going to work," objected Ron. "For a start, Tania can't just drop everything and fail to turn up for work at the library tomorrow."

"I can get Susie, my Number 2, to cover for me," replied Tania. "She's perfectly capable. And Jenny could assist her ..."

Ron couldn't believe his ears. "Jenny? She's only come out of hospital this morning. She's on sick leave."

"Exactly," said Tania. "She certainly can't go back to full-time work at the dental surgery. And she'd be bored to death sitting at home doing nothing, whereas she's quite able to do what she does at the library on Saturdays, sit behind a desk and do nothing but answer phones and check books out. Mild activity is good for convalescents. Just think how chuffed she'd be if she thought she was helping me to solve another murder."

"You're mad, the pair of you," muttered Ron. It was not immediately obvious who he thought the mad pair were.

"And," continued Tania, "I am owed some holiday

time. I bet Susie could clear it with the authorities at County Library headquarters. She can be very persuasive."

"I wonder where she gets that from," grumbled Ron. "And anyway, what about the police? You can't just go barging in. What do you suppose Inspector Copper is going to say if you turn up at his crime scene? He isn't exactly your greatest admirer, is he?"

"Inspector Copper is a pussycat," smiled Tania. "I got him to listen to me at the abbey, didn't I? And anyway, all I'm going to be doing is taking a well-earned break at a friend's farm. The fact that there's been a murder there is just an unfortunate coincidence. And if I happen to get into conversation with the people around the place, well, that's just my chatty nature."

"He'll go off pop," predicted Ron.

"Leave him to me," said Tania. "So what's the situation with him, Leah?"

"He's coming back first thing in the morning. The thing was, for some reason they weren't able to get the forensics people up to the farm today, so what they've done is cordoned off the site to stop anyone going there, and left a constable to keep an eye on things overnight."

"Are you saying that Malcolm is still lying there where you found him?" queried Tania, astonished.

"It surprised me too," admitted Leah. "But the inspector didn't seem to think that any harm would be done. And it does get quite chilly up on the Downs overnight, so they thought that the body wouldn't ... you know."

"Quite," said Ron hastily.

"So what's your suggestion, Leah?" asked Tania.

"I was wondering if there was any way you could get up to the farm this evening," said Leah. "That way, you could settle in and get the lie of the land. And if we can work out a way of doing it, maybe we can get that P.C. out of the way so that you could take a look at the *locus in quo ...*"

"The which?" broke in Ron.

"Sorry. Slipping into barrister-speak," confessed Leah. "And it's a very long time since I did that. Funny how some old habits never quite go away. I mean the scene of the crime. I'm sure there must be some means of getting that young police lad away from the site. Don't they say that a policeman can never resist the lure of a cup of tea?"

"I am surrounded by devious women," said Ron helplessly. "So, love, what do you want to do?"

Tania thought for a moment. "Okay, Leah - it's a deal. Let's see what we can do to help."

"Hmmm. Whatever happened to 'No, no, no!'" murmured Ron rebelliously, before stitching a brave smile on to his features.

"First thing I need to do is get on the phone to Susie," declared Tania. "If she can't fall in with the plan and cover for me, we're scuppered before we start. Then, once I've spoken to her, I'll give Jenny a call and see if she's up for a little light library work for the week."

"If I know Jenny, you'd need wild horses to keep her away," remarked Ron. "But a week? I admire your optimism. But you're the detective."

"Have faith, darling," smiled Tania, depositing a kiss on her husband's nose. "Right. Why don't you pop upstairs and pack some clothes for yourself. I'll get on the phone, and then once I've done that I'll be up to do the same. Oh, Leah," she said, as a sudden thought occurred to her. "What about food. I haven't got a lot in at the moment. Life's been rather hectic lately, what with one thing and another."

"Don't you worry about that," replied Leah. "We've got plenty of food up at the farm. I'll get on to my site manager Mary and get her to open up one of the cottages ready for you. The Byre, I think - that should suit you. And don't fret - there isn't even a whiff of cow left.

And I'll have Mary stock up the fridge. I'll call her from the car." She sprang to her feet. "Well, we'd better all get on with it." She gave Tania a swift hug. "Thank you, my dear. I knew I could rely on you to help. You too, Ron. Well, I'd best be on my way. Things to do. See you in a while." She made for the front door and, as Ron and Tania stood on the threshold, climbed into her Jaguar and, with a roar of exhaust, disappeared up the road.

Chapter 3

"You do realise, love," said Ron, as he slammed the rear door of the couple's hatchback and climbed into the driver's seat, "that you are certifiably insane?"

"More than likely," agreed Tania with an impish smile, as she fastened the passenger seat belt alongside him.

"After all," continued her husband, with a glance at the dashboard clock, "it's a mere twenty-four hours since you were standing in front of the Ramston Literary Society, explaining your brilliant deductions as to who committed a murder in their very midst, no doubt irritating the hell out of that delightful woman detective inspector, and here we are haring off in pursuit of another evildoer."

"Inspector Bright did her best to shoo me away from the case, didn't she?" gurgled Tania in amusement. "But what did she expect me to do? After all, I was personally involved. The whole thing did take place on the library premises, and after Jenny got caught up in it, how could I possibly have just left it alone?"

"I suppose so," nodded Ron. It was true that Tania had already taken a more than passing interest after the sudden and violent death of a prominent member of the Literary Society in Ramston's old library reading room, and following the attack on Jenny Chandler, Tania's part-time Saturday library assistant, it would have been impossible to keep her away from the case. "How is Jenny now, by the way?"

"Surprisingly perky. She was nowhere near as badly hurt as we first feared, and she says the pills the hospital have given her mean that she's in virtually no pain at all. And of course, when I told her what had happened at Leah's farm ..."

"Near Leah's farm," corrected Ron. "She was really most insistent on that, wasn't she?"

"Whatever," said Tania with a dismissive wave of the hand. "Anyway, when I told her about Leah's visit, and that we were off to answer the call of a damsel in distress ..."

"Damsel?" snorted Ron in incredulity. He chuckled. "Leah is about as far away from being a damsel as you can get. I've yet to encounter a damsel wearing dungarees and size nine DMs."

"You know what I mean," said Tania. "Anyway, once I told her what we planned, she couldn't volunteer fast enough. And she promised to sit quietly behind the library front desk and not do anything strenuous. In fact, she was so excited that it was all I could do to persuade her that we didn't need her help looking into things up at the farm."

"Hmmm. Sounds as if Susie's going to have her hands full over the next week," remarked Ron. "And how did she take it when you spoke to her?"

"Actually, she was more than happy to step into my shoes for a few days. After all, she's done it before when I've been on annual leave. And once I'd explained what was going on, she couldn't have been more helpful. She's going to get on to County Library Headquarters first thing in the morning and concoct an utterly plausible cover story about me being in some sort of shock after the Literary Society murder, and so the obvious thing is for me to take a few days' compassionate leave."

"All I can say is, they must have some extremely gullible people at County HQ," said Ron drily. "And as for you and Susie, you seem to make a pretty formidable couple of conspirators. Lord help anyone who gets on the wrong side of you."

"We're a pair of fluffy bunnies," replied Tania with a smug smile. "However, if you don't want to get on the wrong side of me, shouldn't we actually get going? Sitting talking on our drive is going to help nobody, least of all Leah."

"You know your riveting conversation mesmerises me and makes me forget everything else, love," laughed Ron. "But you're right. So let's get you on the trail of another murderer." He switched on the engine, let in the clutch, and turned out of the driveway.

*

Before too long, after a journey without incident on mostly traffic-free Sunday evening main roads, Ron turned off the Westchester bypass and started the long steady climb up towards the high chalk downs above the city. As they continued, the landscape gradually changed. Wide roads gave way to tree-shaded lanes running between a patchwork of neat fields in varying shades of green and gold. In the distance, an occasional cloud of dust arose as a tractor went about its work. The route passed through a scattering of picturesque villages where flint was king, glancing sideways rather snootily at the brick-built parvenu bungalows more recently arrived on the outskirts, and ducks floated in carefree fashion on reed-edged ponds as their ancestors had for centuries. Slowly, the trees began to diminish, and the hedges grew lower, to reveal wide skyscapes populated by towering white clouds.

As the travellers drew nearer to their destination, the road took a dip, and they entered a tree-filled valley, where a roadside sign almost obscured by a flourishing clump of cowslips announced their arrival in Upson Major. A surprisingly large church with a high crenellated tower was almost obscured by a churchyard filled with monumental yew trees, whose branches shaded an extensive range of graves testifying to the village's long history. Simple grey stone slabs, their inscriptions worn to illegibility, stood side by side with elaborate Victorian tombs of granite, marble and wrought-iron, amidst rows of anonymous grass-grown humps dotted with occasional bunches of fading flowers.

In one corner, a patch of freshly-disturbed earth was marked by a simple wooden cross and surmounted by a collection of colourful wreaths and, poignantly, a single teddy bear. The village's main street, a mixture of cottages with flower-filled front gardens and rather grander Georgian houses sheltering behind high brick walls, provided evidence of the locality's importance. A shop front proudly proclaiming its role as 'Family Butchers since 1871' stood alongside 'The Willow Wand – Arts, Crafts and Souvenirs'. 'The Rowan Tree Tearooms' declared that traditional cream teas and home-made cakes were on offer behind the swagged lace curtains adorning its bay window with its ornamental bottle-glass panes. An expanse of plate glass bearing decals of brightly-coloured depictions of the groceries available within announced the existence of 'Upson Community Stores', while across the road a Victorian building with nods to the Gothic bore the title of 'Upson Major Memorial Hall', with a noticeboard telling of 'Yoga on Tuesdays', 'Mothers and Toddlers cancelled next Saturday', and a handwritten poster with a picture of a missing cat.

"Not far to go," observed Ron, as the road emerged from among the trees and took a distinct upward trajectory. Soon the straggling outskirts of Upson Major were left behind, and fields began to give way to areas of open heathland dotted with gorse, with occasional clumps of silver birch. The lane, now reduced to a single track with occasional passing-places, seemed to wriggle before diving into an unexpected tiny tree-filled valley, at whose bottom ran a bubbling stream with a ford which the car splashed through. Emerging with equal suddenness, the skies opened once more, and the first house of Upson Parva appeared. It was accompanied by a scattering of fellows, mostly built in the local flint with brick details under thatched roofs, with the principal building of the hamlet, a substantial structure in pale sandstone, announcing itself in antique script as 'The Drover's Rest - Free House - Ales, Wines and Porter'. And driven into the ground in front of the pub car park's front wall was a modest sign featuring a picture of a tousle-headed animal above the words 'Alpaca Max - half a mile to go'. Moments later, Ron was driving in through the farm gate and into the main yard, pulling up alongside Leah's Jaguar.

As the couple climbed out of the car, Leah emerged from the front door of the farmhouse and advanced towards them. "You took your time," she greeted them. "I was beginning to wonder if you'd got lost."

"We don't all drive like lunatics," protested Ron. "Some of us take a little more care of life and limb."

"She's only teasing, Ron," smiled Tania. "And your driving gives me a perfect opportunity to admire the scenery," she added with a twinkle.

"Yes, dear," replied Ron.

"Anyway, you're here, and I'm very grateful. Did you manage to get everything sorted with work?" enquired Leah.

"All the ducks are happily lined up in a row," said Tania. "I'm at your disposal for the whole week."

"And knowing you, that ought to be more than enough," said Leah. "I have confidence. Now, let's get you settled in. The Byre is over here." She led the way across the farmyard with Tania, while Ron hefted the cases out of the back of the car and followed on.

"Oh, this is charming," said Tania, as Leah threw open the door of the cottage and ushered her guests in. The brick and beams of the living room, with the kitchen beyond, created a warm and welcoming atmosphere, while through another door could be glimpsed an equally cosy bedroom.

"The bathroom's through there," said Leah. "and there's food in the fridge. Anything you need, just ask me or Mary. And I hope you'll be comfortable."

"I'm sure we shall," replied Tania. "However," she said, her expression growing solemn, "we're not exactly here to be comfortable, are we? You've got a problem which you need solved."

"You're not wrong," agreed Leah. "And to be frank, Malcolm was always a problem," she added with grim humour. "But never so much as now."

"You don't seriously think that the police believe you had anything to do with his death, do you?" asked Ron.

Leah shrugged. "At the moment, I don't know what they think. I'm more interested in what you think."

"I don't think anything because I don't know anything," responded Tania reasonably. "I have no facts."

"Well, we'd better let you have some." Leah looked at her watch. "I suppose the first thing is for you to take a look at the scene."

"And the body," put in Ron. "Hadn't we better get a move on? It's not going to stay light forever."

"But Leah, didn't you say that Inspector Copper had left one of his officers on guard at the site?" asked Tania. "He's not going to let us go poking about, is he?"

"Fret not, dearie. I've thought of that." Leah pulled her phone out of her pocket and dialled. "Mary - can you do me a favour? Can you pop up to the barrow with your best sympathetic face on and suggest to that nice young police constable that he must be getting bored, and a cup of tea is exactly what he requires. I just need him away from the site for fifteen minutes ... You're a diamond. I'll leave it with you." She rang off. "Now we just wait a few minutes. Why don't you two unpack while we wait?" She peered out of the cottage door. "There she goes." And shortly afterwards, as Tania and Ron re-emerged from the bedroom, "She's just back, policeman in tow, so the coast's clear. I'll just grab a torch, and off we go."

Through a gate tucked away unobtrusively in one corner of the farmyard, Leah led the way to a path which wound up between fields dotted with grazing animals. As the group reached a hedge at the top of a rise, Tania was amused to see that they were being watched by a cluster of alpacas lined up along the fence, their curly-topped heads reminiscent of nothing so much as a group of fashion-conscious schoolboys.

Leah opened a gate in the hedge. "See?" she said. "This is my property boundary. The barrows are the other side of it. So whatever the press may be saying, not on my land at all."

"You know what journalists are like," sympathised Ron. "They'll never let the truth get in the way of a good story. And they probably think that keeping alpacas is just … weird."

"Weird?" Leah's eyebrows rose to the same extent that her voice dropped to a threatening growl.

"That's because they know nothing about them," intervened Tania hastily. "We know they're utterly lovable, don't we, Ron?"

"Except that cake bandit," muttered Ron under his breath.

Tania affected not to hear. "Anyway," she said brightly, changing the subject, "if it isn't your land beyond the fence, whose is it?"

"It belongs to the government," replied Leah. "Actually, it's quite a sad story. The whole area of the Downs used to be owned by the de la Meres - it was Lord James who originally started the digs at the barrow site over a century ago. But that all stopped during the First World War, and the poor man's only son was killed in the trenches. Then after the war, the family's house Mere Hall over near Westchester caught fire and was burnt to the ground, and in his will Lord de la Mere left his entire estate to the nation. They use some of the land on the far side of the Downs for army exercises, but fortunately, that's miles away from here. I don't think my alpacas would respond very well to the sound of gunfire."

"Just as well there wasn't any shooting involved here then," observed Tania. "I think that's what you said. Because then, somebody might have heard something. But Malcolm was stabbed, didn't you say?"

"You'd better come and see for yourself, hadn't you?" replied Leah. She ushered the couple through the gate, where a faint path led towards a collection of humps in the ground some fifty yards away. As the party grew closer, they could see that there was a group of four round barrows silhouetted against the skyline, while slightly apart, situated in a slight dip, a longer structure was surrounded by evidence of excavation, with a small white tent standing at one side. "Just a second," she said. "They make everyone wear shoe covers inside. I think they're in here." Opening the flap of the tent, she revealed a small table with a pile of blue plastic shoe covers of the type handed out to visitors of fragile historic houses, alongside a heap of surgical gloves and a box of steel trowels. "Better not leave any trace of our presence." Precautions taken, Leah led the others round to one end of the long barrow where, behind a police tape and at the foot of some roughly-dug steps, a makeshift doorway had been constructed, consisting of a wooden framework with a tarpaulin sheet across the opening. "This is the way in. You'll need the torch."

Tania carefully pulled aside the tarpaulin and, with Ron at her side, stepped into the darkened interior. She switched on the torch and waited for a moment as her eyes adjusted to the gloom, bending almost double to avoid the low ceiling. There before her ran the low central passage-way of the barrow, with dim openings to the left and right. And ahead, at the far end, in the entrance to what was evidently a further chamber at the end, lay the sprawled body of a man. He wore jeans, and a checked shirt of an indeterminate colour with, Tania was faintly surprised to notice, plastic over-shoes of the type she was wearing. His head with its shock of white hair was turned to the right, and the wide-open eyes and expression of utter surprise on the features told of the suddenness of his end. A hand-torch lay alongside him, the dim flicker of its bulb testament to an almost-expired battery charge. His right hand was stretched out in front of him as if to grasp some object. Next to the outstretched hand, a shiny steel excavator's trowel. And in the centre of his back, a wide slit in the fabric of the shirt, surrounded by a large bloodstain.

"Well, there he is," murmured Leah, who had entered unobserved behind the couple. "Poor Malcolm."

"But what was he doing here?" wondered Tania. "And by all accounts, in the middle of the night. And why ... and who ..."

"That's what I was hoping you could tell me," said Leah. "We may not always have seen eye to eye, but he never deserved this. Although," she added darkly, "for an archaeologist, it's probably where he would have wanted to end up."

"Seen enough, love?" asked Ron. "Because all this crouching is doing my back no good at all. And it's not as if we can touch anything, or we'll be in deep trouble with your friend Inspector Copper. Not only that, but I dare say that police constable chappie isn't going to be sat sipping tea down at the farm forever."

"You're right," agreed Tania. "We should go. But ... that wound. It's too wide for an ordinary knife." Her gaze ranged around the scene. "But what about that trowel ..."

Ron peered. "Except there doesn't seem to be any blood on it," he pointed out.

"True," admitted Tania. She cast one last look at the dead man. "I'll do my best, Malcolm," she murmured in a low voice, before turning and following the others out into the gathering twilight.

Chapter 4

"Right, love," said Ron, as he deposited a cup of tea on his wife's bedside table before climbing back into bed alongside her. "Now that we're rested and refreshed - and by the way, who knew the countryside was so quiet at night? - what's the cunning plan? I assume you have one."

Tania reflected for a moment. "I suppose the first thing to do is to find out who's involved. If what Leah told us is right, then it's only the dig people and her staff who could possibly be in the frame."

"I take it we're ruling out the alpacas?"

Tania shot her husband a sideways look. "I was hoping you were going to be helpful, darling."

Ron grinned unrepentantly. "I'm just taking a leaf out of Sherlock Holmes' book. You know - get rid of the impossible, and what's left must be true. Somebody stabbed Malcolm. And with the alpacas, I'm thinking the lack of opposable thumbs ..."

Despite herself, Tania couldn't help laughing as she gave Ron a good-natured swat. "I'd be very grateful if that turns out to be the last of your half-witted Watsonisms in this case." She grew serious. "And it's not just the matter of seeing if we can find out who's responsible for the murder. I'm concerned about Leah. For all her usual robustness, I can tell she's worried deep down. If the police take it into their heads to regard her as a possible murderer, goodness knows how that might affect her. Not to mention the effect on her livelihood. If the rumours start spreading and the cancellations keep coming, how's her business going to survive?"

"You're right, love," said Ron, sobered. "So, back to what I said. What's the cunning plan?"

"We make a list. Probably several."

"*Dramatis personae*, so to speak, for a start."

"Exactly. Who are the people involved in the

archaeological dig, who are the people who work for Leah, and who was where when? Suspects and witnesses, in fact. And the best way to get answers to all that is to talk to people."

"Which is your forté, love. Although surely there are going to be a few raised eyebrows if we start interrogating suspects and witnesses alongside the police."

"And that, darling, is where the cunning plan comes in," replied Tania. "We are not interrogating anybody. We just happen to be old friends of Leah's who have come to stay with her for a long-planned break. But what a horrible coincidence it is that this should have coincided with a murder! Our dear friend must be devastated! As must they. So, sympathy in bucketfuls. 'Were you close to the dead man? How on earth could such a thing have come about? What do you think?' I can do gossipy," she concluded with a satisfied smile.

Ron leaned across to give his wife a peck on the cheek. "And nobody with any knowledge of your outstanding acting abilities at R.O.A.D.S. would doubt it for a second, love. I can't wait to see you in action. But in the meantime, I have a cunning plan of my own."

"Which is ...?"

"To leap forth, carry out some swift ablutions, and then rustle up some breakfast while you make yourself extra beautiful. And then we'll venture out and make a start. As I'm sure somebody once said, the game's afoot." Ron climbed out of bed and headed for the bathroom.

*

As the couple emerged from The Byre, they were just in time to see an anonymous small white van drive into the farmyard. The vehicle disgorged two women who opened the rear doors before proceeding to don white overalls. As the pair collected what looked like substantial plastic toolboxes from the back of the van, their vehicle was followed into the yard by a sleek black saloon, from which emerged two suited individuals.

"Well, well," murmured Ron. "Here are two familiar faces. Detective Inspector Copper and Detective Sergeant Radley, if I'm not very much mistaken."

"Which you aren't," replied Tania in similarly lowered tones. She let out a resigned sigh. "Oh no."

The leading police officer, a stocky man looking to be in his late thirties, a little above medium height, and with a friendly expression on a face topped by a semi-tamed mop of tousled hair, had casually glanced around the farmyard, only to come to a sudden halt as his eye fell on Tania and Ron. His shoulders slumped slightly, before he straightened up with a determined air and advanced on the couple, his somewhat younger and chubbier colleague in his wake.

"Mrs Faye," he said, his features wearing a rather tight smile. "Now here's a face I didn't expect to see. Or rather, shouldn't have expected to see." He let out a slightly resigned chuckle. "Or should I?"

"Inspector Copper," replied Tania brightly. "I really don't know what you mean. But how nice to see you again. I hope you enjoyed your firearms course."

"How the ...?" Copper stopped abruptly and laughed. "Of course. Ramston's leading amateur sleuth has eyes and ears everywhere. Including, I gather from my colleagues at the station, in your own library. Very recently, I hear. So I'm wondering how on earth you come to be here at the scene of another ... 'incident', shall we say?"

"Oh inspector, isn't it just the most awful coincidence?" replied Tania, wide-eyed. "Who could have had any idea that something like this would happen so near to Leah's farm? You see, she's a very old and dear friend, and she'd invited Ron and me to come and stay with her in her holiday cottages for a little break - oh, ages ago. So after all the excitement of last week, we thought we'd come and take her up on her invitation. I've heard so much about the alpacas, so I couldn't wait to meet them. Of course, we never imagined ... well, you know."

Copper gave the librarian a long level look. "Mrs Faye," he said after a considerable pause. "I was not born yesterday. And you know my views on outside involvement in a police investigation. However helpful," he pressed on, as Tania seemed to be about to interrupt, "that involvement may have been on a previous occasion. So please, whatever your intentions may be, leave us to do our work. And enjoy your holiday. You too, Mr Faye."

"Of course, inspector," responded Tania with suspicious meekness. "I would never dream of interfering. I'm just here to relax and have a pleasant time."

Copper favoured Tania with a final look, eyebrow quirked as he let out a resigned sigh, before turning to his colleague. "Come along, Radley. Let's start Forensics on the case before the day gets any older." The pair of officers moved across to the two overall-clad women, who had been watching the encounter with interest, and after a brief exchange, punctured with occasional glances back towards the Fayes, the group headed for the gate in the corner of the farmyard and disappeared in the direction of the dig site.

"Well, that's us told," remarked Ron. "I think we may have to pull our horns in a bit."

"Not a chance!" retorted Tania robustly. "There's a mystery here, and a friend to help. No way am I going to be put off. Come on - let's go and see Leah and make a start on our lists."

*

Ron's hand had scarcely left the knocker of the farmhouse door when it was flung wide by Leah.

"I saw you talking to the inspector," said the Scotswoman by way of greeting.

"Yes," responded Tania. "That was an unexpected pleasure. I never anticipated that our paths would cross quite so soon."

"Problem?" enquired a concerned-looking Leah.

"No, not at all," said Ron with a smile. "He was just warning Tania off, in the most charming way possible. He indicated that any interference by her in his investigation would not be appreciated in the slightest."

"So are you going to do what he says?"

"When pigs fly!" laughed Tania. "Or maybe in this case, I ought to say 'alpacas'. No, you asked for our help, and that's what you're going to get, whatever Inspector Copper may prefer. Of course, I explained to him that we're just old friends of yours here for a nice relaxing break, but he didn't buy that for a second. Let's face it, he wouldn't be much of a detective if he had. So don't worry on that score."

"I won't," said Leah. "I've got other things to worry about. Like, did he mention me at all? I have a feeling he's got his beady eye on me, for all that I told him that I'd had virtually nothing to do with Malcolm for years, so why would I have a reason to do him harm? That's why I didn't come out when I saw you talking to him."

"I don't think you need to fret overmuch about what the inspector is thinking at the moment," observed Ron. "From what we've seen of him, he's a pretty reasonable chap, and he's not going to be pursuing any thoughts without evidence to back them up. That's the way it was with the business at Ramston Abbey. He wasn't over-fond of the evidence Tania laid out for him, but he was fair in the way he looked at it."

"And he'll do the same when Tania has found the solution to this case, I'm hoping," said Leah.

"Which is why we've come knocking," said Tania. "We'd better make a start on finding out the who, where, and when. Especially the who."

"Of course, of course. And here I am keeping you standing on the doorstep. For goodness sake, come on in and I'll put the kettle on."

"Brilliant idea," smiled Ron. "Nothing like a cuppa for kick-starting the little grey cells into action."

With the three installed in the farmhouse's cosy beamed sitting room, a tray of tea-things on the coffee table in front of the huge inglenook fireplace, Leah looked expectantly at Tania. "So where do you want to begin?"

"I suppose with the people in and around the farm," responded Tania. "You said you have people who work for you."

"I do, Not that many, fortunately. We're a happy few, because the alpacas look after themselves to a great extent. I suppose the one who handles most of the responsibility is my manager, Mary."

Tania produced a small notebook. "And that would be Mary ...?"

"Mary Winterbourne."

Tania jotted down the name. "So where does Mary fit into the farm?"

Leah gave the ghost of a fond smile. "I couldn't run the place without her. She's a godsend."

"Known her long?"

"Not all that long, actually. A few years. It's a bit of a long story. We got chatting over a drink at some event or other, and I was in need of a manager, and she wanted a change of career, so things sort of fell into place."

"And what does she do?"

"She's mostly in charge of bookings. That's bookings for the holiday cottages, as well as the appointments for visitors who come to the farm for the alpaca experiences - you know, the walks and the picnics. And she helps prepare the cottages when there's a changeover of guests. By the way, how's The Byre? Are you comfortable? Do you have everything you need?"

"It couldn't be better," answered Ron. "We were as snug as a bug in a rug last night."

"And does Mary live on site?" wondered Tania. "I would imagine she would need to."

"Aye. She stays in the Old Piggery. Which is much nicer than it sounds. And it's just close to her office in the Tack Room."

"Right. Got that. So, you say she helps with the cottage changeovers, which implies that there's somebody else involved. Who would that be?" enquired Tania.

"That's Jane - Jane Sherrington. She does the cleaning for me, and all the laundry and whatnot."

"And does she also live in"

"Och no. She only works for me part-time. There's not enough work to justify a full-time employee. And anyway, she's got a proper job at the pub."

"That would be the Drover's Rest in the village, I assume," put in Ron. "We passed it on the way up here."

"That's right," agreed Leah. "She's the barmaid there. Nice woman."

"Now there's a potentially useful source of information," remarked Ron. "Barmaids always know everything. A swift jar at the pub at some time, I think."

"So she's local?" asked Tania.

"Aye. She stays at the pub. She's got a flat there. She lives there with Henry."

"Henry? Who's Henry?"

"That's Henry Gifford, my other full-timer. We call him the alpaca-wrangler."

"I think I can guess what that means," smiled Tania. "So presumably he's in charge of the animals' welfare, and organising things when your visitors take them for walks and so on."

"That's exactly it," said Leah. "I know I said the beasts don't need that much looking after, but when they do, Henry's the man. There's nothing he doesn't know about them."

"And has he been with you long?"

"He came the day the alpacas arrived," replied Leah. "It was a sort of package deal. I bought the first couple of beasts from another farm, and Henry came as a temporary measure, just to see that they settled in. But then he found he liked it here, so he became a fixture and he's never left. And he gets on so well with the kids who come visiting. I couldn't ask for better."

"And that's it as regards staff?"

"It is. There's just the outsiders."

"You mean the people involved with the dig."

"Yes. We didn't have anyone else staying in the holiday cottages on Saturday night."

"Well, that's one potential complication avoided," said Tania in relief. "So, who are these dig people?"

"I can't really tell you a lot about them," said Leah. "Mostly I only know the names. They're pretty much all from Camford University, so I'd never met any of them before."

"So I'll just make a note of the names, and then I can have a chat with each of them as we go. They will obviously all have had some sort of contact with Malcolm. Let's see if we can find out any kind of motivation among them."

"There's the man in charge, Edward Wilton," began Leah. "Well, he's obviously in charge now, I imagine. He's a professor at Camford. He was Malcolm's second-in-command, although I get the impression that he rather thought he ought to have been in charge in the first place."

"Ah, we love a bit of jealousy," grinned Ron. "Makes a perfect motive for dastardly deeds."

"Then there are the three students," continued Leah. "Well, I say students, but you might not think they all fit the description. Two of them are youngsters, that's Victoria Whaddon and Stephen Tisbury. Twenty-ish or thereabouts, I believe. And if I'm not much mistaken, from what little I've seen, I've a feeling that young Steve has something of a soft spot for Victoria, but you'd better not quote me."

"And the third?"

"That's Anne - Anne Langford. Looks more like a teacher than a student, but apparently she's what they call a 'mature student'. Same sort of age as me, I'm guessing, so I suppose that makes me a 'mature farmer'." A dry self-deprecating smile. "Anne's something of a mother hen to the two kids. I think she feels a bit protective towards them."

"So is that it?" asked Tania.

"No, there's one more," said Leah.

"Another one from Camford?"

"No, actually he's another local. George Cheverell from the village. He's some sort of amateur historian, and it seems he heard about the dig and volunteered his services. I don't actually know him - he's never been up to the farm for any of the activities."

"And to your knowledge, had any of these people ever come into contact with Malcolm before the start of the excavations here?"

Leah shook her head. "Not that I know of."

Tania pondered for a moment. "So, whatever led to Malcolm's death must have happened in the period since the group came together."

"And your brilliant acting skills are going to come in very handy when you engage in innocent conversation with all these people," remarked Ron. "I take it, Leah, that none of them are aware of Tania's sleuthing pedigree?"

"No," said Leah. "I only told Mary that you're old friends of mine who have come to stay and offer me a bit of moral support. Nobody else knows a thing."

"Then we shall keep it that way," declared Tania. "And I might as well make a start sooner rather than later. I'd better begin with Mary, if you can tell me where

I'm likely to find her."

"Just across the yard in her office in the Tack Room," said Leah. "I'll point it out to you."

The three rose, and Leah led the way to the front door. On opening it, they found that a black van with the legend 'Private Ambulance' had joined the other vehicles in the farmyard, and two sombrely-dressed individuals were loading a stretcher bearing a black plastic body bag into the back, while the two police detectives and the pair of white-overall-clad women stood by watching. Doors were slammed, and the van drove out of the farmyard, followed by the small white van belonging to the forensic team. After a moment Inspector Copper, with a lingering meaningful glance in the direction of Tania and Ron as they stood silently watching, made his way over to the group and addressed Leah.

"Mrs Sutherland," he said, "as far as my investigations are concerned, the excavation site is clear. You may inform your guests that they may resume their activities at the barrow. Your archaeological guests, that is." He flicked a glance at Tania. "As for your other - 'guests' - I think I have made my position clear to them."

"Of course, inspector. I quite understand," said Tania. "Oh - just one question, if I may. I assume your forensic colleagues have examined the body for cause of death. So just a single wide stab wound, was it? From something triangular like ... oh, I don't know ... an excavator's trowel? Perhaps penetrating the heart?"

"And how, I wonder, would you know that, Mrs Faye?" growled Copper.

"I must have heard it somewhere," replied Tania airily. "Was it on the TV, perhaps?"

Copper gave her a long level look before turning wordlessly on his heel. He climbed into his own car, accompanied by his sergeant and the young uniformed officer from the dig site, and followed in the wake of the other vehicles.

Chapter 5

"Come in!" The brisk reply came in response to Tania's knock at the door marked 'Office' in one of the range of outbuildings surrounding the farmyard.

Tania pushed open the door and popped her head around it. "Sorry to disturb you. I hope it's not an inconvenient moment."

Mary Winterbourne rose from behind her desk with a friendly smile. "Not at all. Do come in." Tania and Ron were quick to accept the invitation and, in response to Mary's gesture, seated themselves in the pair of chairs in front of her desk. "And what can I do for you?"

"Oh no, it's what we can do," replied Tania. "You see, I'm Tania Faye and this is my husband Ron, and we just wanted to thank you for organising the wonderful little cottage you've arranged for us at such short notice. It's so charming and comfortable."

Ron, alongside his wife, was straining every nerve to avoid laughing at his wife's expert characterisation of a twittery housewife.

"Oh, it's my pleasure," said Mary. "Although it's Leah you ought to be thanking. It was her idea. I just did the donkey work. I gather you're old friends of hers?"

"That's right," said Ron. "And it all came out of the blue really. You see," he continued, improvising rapidly, "Tania's had something of a stressful week, what with … one thing and another. Do you by any chance watch the local news?"

Mary snorted. "I try to keep away from the news completely if I possibly can. It's never good, from what I can tell. Mostly people trying their best to kill other people in far-off parts of the world, or else our own politicians never giving a straight answer to any question they get asked. Why?"

"Oh, I just wondered. It's just that there's been a bit of trouble where Tania works, so she needed a break, and Leah came up with this idea of our enjoying a few days here at the farm. I gather that spending time with your alpacas is a very restful business."

"Hmmm." Mary's mouth turned down in a grimace. "A restful business is what we seem to be stuck with at the moment, if the last twenty-four hours is anything to go by."

"Really? How so?" asked Tania, portraying wide-eyed surprise.

"But you must know," said Mary. "About the murder, I mean."

"Oh yes," replied Tania. "Leah did tell us about it. And her ex-husband too, which seems the oddest thing. But it wasn't anything to do with the farm, was it? I mean, nothing actually took place on your premises, did it?"

"We only know that because Leah wanted us to go up last night and see the site where it all happened," explained Ron. "We weren't all that keen, to be honest, but Leah insisted. But I don't see why it would affect your business."

"Because," said Mary, "any talk connecting us and the murder has the most dreadful knock-on effect. That's one of the things I dislike most about the media. Give them a tiny snippet, and everything's blown up out of all proportion. Anti-social media, I call them. I won't even have a smartphone. I have a brick. But start a rumour that there's something going on up here, and suddenly nobody wants to have anything to do with us. I spent half my time yesterday answering the phone to panicking people who were cancelling bookings for cottages or alpaca visits." She sighed. "So it's actually a nice change to have somebody normal about the place."

"But you've got the people associated with the archaeological dig staying here, didn't Leah say?" said Tania. "Aren't they normal?"

"Oh, of course, I didn't mean that," responded

Mary with a slightly forced laugh. "No, they're probably all very nice. Not that I've had a great deal to do with them - well, most of them. I just meant that to have somebody who is here for a regular holiday break, keeping normal hours, is something of a change from the dig people. But I expect you'll probably meet them about the place from time to time."

"And tell me," said Tania, adopting her most sincere and sympathetic tone, "did you have much in the way of contact with Leah's poor ex-husband - Malcolm, wasn't it?"

A certain stiffness entered Mary's manner. "Not really."

"But he was the leader of the expedition, wasn't he?" persisted Tania. "So I expect he would have been in to see you if there was anything that needed to be organised regarding the accommodation or catering or anything like that."

"I suppose so." Mary's reluctance was plain.

"But you weren't exactly friends, is that it? You didn't socialise?"

"Well, of course, our paths did cross once or twice when the group were down at the Drover's when I happened to be there," said Mary.

"So you must have been shocked when he turned up dead. And upset too, I imagine. I dare say all the group were."

"I would think so," replied Mary, a little more confidently. "As I say, I haven't really had time to mix with them all that much."

"And I must say that I admire you for the way you've carried on, under the circumstances. Like Leah. I think she's being very brave. Of course, she's always been a strong character."

"You've known her a long time, haven't you?" enquired Mary, seemingly happy to change the subject. "How did you meet?"

"Oh gosh, that was ages ago," said Tania. "But certainly after she and Malcolm had split up, so we never met him. Which is a shame, because we don't actually know what sort of man he was, and I feel a little awkward asking Leah. And as you say, you didn't really know him, so it's not as if I can ask you for a character description, is it?" A bright smile.

"No," responded Mary shortly.

"I shall just have to tread delicately and try to worm it out of Leah," smiled Tania. "I shall trade on our long friendship of however-many-it-is years." She turned to her husband. "Ron, can you remember when we first knew her?"

"I can," replied Ron. "It was when she came to direct a production of 'Whoops, There Go My Trousers!' for R.O.A.D.S. Now there's a play you couldn't do these days," he remarked. "You'd have the Woke Police down on you like a ton of bricks." He turned back to Mary. "We're with the Ramston Operatic And Dramatic Society," he explained. "Tania and I have been members forever, and Leah came to the society as a director. Very successfully, I might add. She's very talented. And she can turn her hand to almost anything – set design, carpentry, costume making. I don't know how she manages to fit it all in with running the farm. She's brilliant at comedy, but she can do practically anything. She has a specially deft touch with Shakespeare."

"She directed Ron and me in the leads when we did our open-air production of 'A Midsummer Night's Dream' a little while ago," said Tania.

"Wait," interrupted Mary. "Was that the show where she was away in Cornwall for a week?"

"Er … actually, yes," said Ron. "I expect she was glad of you being here to run the place in her absence."

"No, that's not what I mean," said Mary. "Didn't I hear that there was a murder at some point during the play?"

"Now you come to mention it, yes," admitted Tania. "But it wasn't anything to do with any of our company. It turned out to involve a local."

"Less 'Midsummer Night's Dream', more 'Love's Labour's Lost'," remarked Ron in an attempt at humour.

"But I seem to remember Leah saying something about it, and how one of your theatre company was instrumental in solving the crime." Mary's eyes narrowed as she regarded Tania. "Was that you?"

"Not really," said Tania evasively. "I mean, I might have mentioned one or two things I'd noticed to the police, but they were the ones who arrested the culprit."

Mary's demeanour changed. "And now we have a murder here, and Leah invites you along for a holiday. And here you are, asking questions. Some people might think that was too much of a coincidence."

"Oh, I assure you," said Tania, wide-eyed and innocent, "I don't have the slightest intention of getting mixed up in anything to do with Malcolm Sutherland's death. After all, the police are on the case, and they're the experts. I just want to support Leah. And to have a little holiday."

"Well, I hope you enjoy it," said Mary, an unconvincing smile on her face. Her phone rang. "And now, if you'll excuse me, I'd better take this. It's probably somebody else cancelling their booking. News travels far and fast."

"Of course. We'll get out of your way. And thank you for your time." Ron ducked his head in apology as he stood and held Tania's chair for her. As the couple exited the Tack Room, they could hear Mary saying "Good morning. Alpaca Max … Mr Robinson. How are you? … Broken in two places? How awful … No, of course you can't be expected to come …"

The door closed behind them.

*

"Oops," said Ron.

"Yes," said Tania ruefully. "That could have gone better."

"Oh, I don't know," responded Ron. "I was admiring your flawless portrayal of a chatty gossip."

"Until I went and put my big foot in it by mentioning our production of 'Dream'," said Tania. "I must say, Mary was pretty quick off the mark to put two and two together and realise exactly who I was. She's evidently no fool. Which could cause complications."

"Why so?"

"Well, she's obviously on our suspects list. She would certainly have had the opportunity to be in the right place and time to kill Malcolm. As for means, there's no mystery in that. I should think the archaeological site is dotted with trowels of the sort we saw. We've seen enough programmes on TV to know that's what practically everybody uses during a dig, so I doubt if we'll be able to identify a particular user, even if we had the trowel in our possession. And I'm certain Inspector Copper isn't going to let us get our hands on it." A wry smile.

"Although," pointed out Ron, "you did get him to virtually admit that a trowel was the only show in town when it came to the actual killing. Even if not the one we saw."

"Yes, he wasn't exactly happy about that, was he?" smiled Tania. "I'm sure he realised that we'd sneaked up there to take a look at the murder scene. That young P.C. probably mentioned that he'd been lured away last night. Not that we touched anything up there, so he can't come after us on that score. But we don't want to get on the wrong side of him, or he might be thinking in terms of charging us with impeding a police investigation."

"Whereas you," grinned Ron, "are filled with an innocent desire to stay out of his way. Mind you, if any helpful information happens to fall into your lap ..."

"I would be failing in my civic duty if I didn't pass it on." Tania responded with an answering grin. The grin faded. "But getting back to Mary, I think we may have made things more difficult for ourselves. She's certainly not going to be as forthcoming as we'd wish. And I'm sure that there was some kind of situation going on between her and Malcolm."

"Absolutely," agreed Ron. "She tensed up whenever you asked about her relationship with him. But whether that means there was something going on which turned sour, or whether he got on the wrong side of her from the start and things escalated to an unfortunate conclusion, we'll just have to winkle out as best we may."

"At least one good thing," remarked Tania. "She did say that she has very little to do with the archaeological party, so that should mean that she won't go blowing our cover as far as they're concerned. We'll just have to hope that she's not the gossipy sort with the other staff."

"So," said Ron, drawing a breath. "What next?"

Tania thought for a moment. "Speaking of the archaeological party, I don't see why we shouldn't take a little saunter up there, now that Inspector Copper has declared the site open again. A little natural curiosity may bring rewards."

"Sounds good to me," nodded Ron. "Let's go." He led the way towards the gate leading to the path upwards.

*

The path led between paddocks bordered with hedges in which the occasional birch or rowan shed a patch of dappled shade. The fields were dotted with grazing alpacas of various colours and in different sizes, and as the couple passed, one of the creatures raised its head, gave them an inquisitive look, and trotted over in their direction. They stopped to meet it and, as it arrived, it gave a soft bleat of greeting.

"This seems a friendly little chap," said Ron. "Do you suppose it's one of the animals they use for the walks?"

"He certainly seems used to people," replied Tania. "That's if it is a 'he', of course."

"Can't help you there, love," said Ron. "I'm afraid my knowledge of alpaca anatomy doesn't run to telling the difference, and I certainly don't intend to go rummaging about at the back end to find out. I'm happy to remain in blissful ignorance. In fact, I'm planning on remaining a respectful distance from the front end as well. Haven't I heard that these animals have a highly unpleasant habit of spitting?"

Tania chuckled. "I think you're confusing them with llamas. They're the ones with the particularly bad habit, or so I've heard. Easy mistake to make, I suppose. Alpacas, llamas, vicuñas – they're all South American camelids. Come to that, camels have some pretty disgusting personal habits as well."

Ron gazed at his wife with raised eyebrows. "And when did you become an expert on South American wildlife? Have you been keeping something from me?"

"Not at all," laughed Tania. "Don't forget, darling, you married a librarian. What do you think I do in the few blessed moments of quietness in the library? Answer – I browse idly through reference books. You never know when some snippet or other is going to come in useful."

"My mistake," said Ron in mock apology. "And thank you for the information. I'm so pleased for Leah that she keeps alpacas instead of llamas."

"How so?" queried Tania.

"Because," gurgled Ron, "then she'd be a llama farmer!"

"Idiot!" Tania aimed a playful swat at her husband.

"Anyway," he continued, "I shall now be quite

happy to make friends with our little chum here." He extended a hand warily, to which the animal gave a tentative sniff before gazing back at Ron.

"Oh, look at those lovely huge brown eyes," exclaimed Tania in admiration. "And as for those eyelashes, I wouldn't mind betting that there are loads of women who would happily kill to have eyelashes like that."

"Hmmm. Not the most convincing motive for murder I've ever heard." Ron's face grew solemn. "Which reminds me that we're on the hunt for an actual motive for murder. And standing around chatting to an alpaca, however loveable, isn't going to get the babby washed, as my old granny used to say."

"You're right," agreed Tania. "We'd better leave our new friend and carry on with our research."

"Ever the librarian," muttered Ron, as the pair resumed their climb.

As they passed through the gate in the hedge which marked Leah's property boundary, the whole vista of Upson Downs opened before them. The sky, a milky blue punctuated with clouds drifting in a leisurely procession from horizon to horizon, seemed to stretch forever. In the far distance, a pair of circling birds which Ron surmised could be buzzards were drifting slowly upwards in a thermal spiral, while nearer at hand could be heard the thrusting warble of a skylark as it celebrated its rise from its nest into the clear air.

"Very Vaughan Williams," murmured Tania.

"And I know it probably sounds stupid, but I've never seen skies this big," breathed a slightly awestruck Ron. "It makes you wonder what the prehistoric inhabitants were thinking when they lived here."

"And died here," responded Tania in a soft voice. "Was there somebody up there who had created all this? Did they lay their people to rest here to be closer to their gods?"

The pair lowered their gaze to take in the monuments close by. The four round barrows, serene grass-covered humps, stood a little way to one side, while slightly apart lay the long barrow, with an entirely different air about it. The police tape had gone, and there was evidence of excavation all around the entrance, where the surface earth had been scraped back. Outside the entrance, kneeling on the chalk surface with its thin covering of remaining soil could be seen the back of an individual with flaming red hair, who was apparently engaged in revealing a further layer. The tarpaulin which had covered the entrance on the couple's first visit had been tied to one side, and from within the barrow could be heard faint sounds of conversation.

"So what's the difference between a round barrow and a long barrow?" wondered Ron. "I have to confess that my entire knowledge of barrows comes from reading that bit in 'Lord Of The Rings' about the barrow-wight."

"Not exactly a master-class in prehistoric archaeology," chuckled Tania. "Basically, they're all burial mounds."

"And do you propose to tell me all about them with the knowledge gleaned from your afore-mentioned reference-book browsing?" enquired Ron with a smile.

"Kindly do not mock, darling," responded Tania. "You never know when something is going to come in handy. As far as I can remember, the long barrows came first, and round barrows are later. But don't quote me."

"What about that Saxon ship burial in East Anglia?"

"Ah. Slightly different animal. Lots of those around Scandinavia. The Vikings had their own set of practices, and I think they kept them going for longer. But I don't know if that's what we've got here. Tell you what," suggested Tania. "Why don't we stop speculating and go and find someone who can actually tell us what this dig is all about? And don't forget, we're witless friends of Leah's who are staying at the farm and who've come rubber-necking. We know nothing. Do you think you can pretend total ignorance, darling."

"Shouldn't be a problem, love," replied Ron. "As you so often tell me, dearest," he added, just loud enough for Tania to hear. "Er ... excuse me!" he hailed the figure who was working at the barrow entrance.

The figure straightened, to reveal a gangly young man with a trowel in his hand and a smudge of earth on one cheek. "Yes? Can I help you?"

Ron stepped forward. "We're staying at the farm, and we heard about the dig. It all sounds fascinating, so we wondered if someone could tell us about it."

"Oh, right. You'd better have a word with Professor Wilton." The young man stepped forward to the barrow entrance and called inside. "Professor, can you spare a moment? There's someone here who'd like to speak to you."

Chapter 6

After a few seconds, a middle-aged man emerged through the doorway into the barrow brushing dust from the knees of his trousers, removed the blue plastic covers from his shoes, peeled off his lightweight rubber gloves, and approached Tania and Ron. "Were you wanting me? What can I do for you?" he enquired guardedly.

Tania paused for a few seconds before uttering, in a voice of delighted amazement, "Oh goodness! It's you, isn't it?"

Ron, at her side, looked momentarily baffled, before realising that his wife was entering into one of her dramatic characterisations, and then swiftly relaxing his features into something neutral while waiting to see what Tania had in mind. He didn't have long to wait.

"I'm right, aren't I?" continued his wife. "I've seen you on television, haven't I? On that programme ... oh Ron, what's it called?"

"Er ..."

"'Digging Up Britain'! That's it, isn't it?" gushed Tania. "Well, goodness, I never expected to meet an actual celebrity today."

"Oh, hardly that, madam." The man managed to squeeze a reply into Tania's verbal flow.

"I think you are," declared Tania robustly. "I remember watching that programme and thinking that I'd never heard our history explained so clearly before. I mean, I've read a little, but I never knew who the Beaker Folk were before seeing you telling us all about them. So thank you."

The man seemed a little nonplussed at the praise being heaped upon him. "You're very kind, madam. And you are ...?

"Oh, I'm so sorry. I should have said. I'm Tania Faye, and this is my husband Ron. We're staying at the alpaca farm just down the hill. We're hoping to do some alpaca walks in the week. And I know it's awful, but I can't actually remember your name. I know it's Professor something ..."

"Wilton - Edward Wilton."

"And aren't you in charge of the archaeological department at Camford University?"

"That's right. Well remembered," said Edward.

"So lovely to meet you," smiled Tania effusively. "I wonder, if it's not an awful imposition, if you could tell us something about what you're doing here. It looks absolutely fascinating. The lady who runs the farm told us there was some sort of archaeological investigation going on up here, but of course she didn't know the details. That's if you can spare the time, of course."

Edward gave a small condescending smile. "I don't see why not. I'm sure I can spare a few minutes for one of my fans. Or, I hope, two." A dry chuckle. "So what would you like to know?"

"Well, for a start," said Ron, "I can see that you're working on the large earthwork here, and there's that group of other mounds just over there. Is that for a particular reason, or did you just think that the biggest one was probably the most important?"

Edward drew himself up a little and adopted what Tania deduced was his standard lecturing posture. "Actually, Mr Faye, it's a little of both. But the round barrows you can see over there - we call them 'tumuli', 'tumulus' in the singular, in the archaeological world, but I don't want to blind you with technicalities - they have already been fairly comprehensively excavated a century or so ago by the then land-owner. There were a few finds, but nothing too spectacular, apart from a rather fine Bronze Age dagger, which is on display in the County Museum. However, at that time, the long barrow was not included in the investigation because the First World War intervened. But recently-discovered documents had re-ignited interest in the long barrow, and the University of Camford decided to get involved, so that's why we're here. We're hoping to do better."

"And do all these ... 'tumuli'? Am I saying that right? ... date from the same period?" enquired Tania.

"Ah!" The professor's eyes sparkled. "You're very astute, Mrs Faye. Because that was what was thought at first. However, it transpires that the long barrow is much later. We've found some items which may well place it in what the popular press are pleased to call, in their uneducated way, 'The Dark Ages'. In other words, post-Roman, pre-Conquest."

"How wonderful," breathed Tania. "Can you tell us what you've found, or is it a closely guarded secret?" She favoured the professor with an impish smile.

Edward chuckled. "Not at all, Mrs Faye. Although I'd probably prefer if you didn't go broadcasting the details on your social media until I've had a chance to publish the paper which I shall certainly be writing at the end of our work. But I see no reason why you shouldn't take a look at what we've found, although I wouldn't get my hopes too high if I were you. Things that excite archaeologists are very often just odd bits of pot or bone to the general public. We haven't come across any great treasures so far, although we still have a way to go. But if you're interested, we have our finds spread out in one of the old barns down at the farm. I could certainly let one of our team show them to you."

"That would be lovely," said Tania. "And I don't suppose ..." She ventured hesitantly.

"Do go on."

"I don't suppose we could just have the tiniest peep to see where you're working inside. I mean, we wouldn't want to disturb anything or interfere with your work."

"I think we can allow just a small glance," replied Edward expansively, evidently won over by Tania's fulsome flattery. "Although I will have to ask you to wear some rather unflattering foot covers so as not to affect the contents of the interior."

"No problem," said Ron, and the couple followed the professor to the tent, all donning shoe covers before continuing to the barrow entrance and peering into the interior, dimly lit by a lantern hanging from the ceiling..

"This is where the work is taking place," explained Edward. "We've already exposed two chambers on either side of this central corridor, and that's where the finds we have so far have come from."

"Edward, are you back?" A head popped out of one of the side chambers. "Oh. I didn't know we had visitors."

"Nothing to worry your little head about, Anne," said Edward. "Just you carry on with what you're doing." He turned back to Tania and Ron. "Now we've made a start on what we believe to be the main chamber at the far end, where George is working." He gestured towards a shadowy individual barely visible in the gloom. "Early days, of course, but we have hopes, although there may be signs that the chamber may have been interfered with, possibly in antiquity ... well, I'd probably better not say any more."

"Treasure, you mean?" asked Tania, wide-eyed. "Gold?"

Edward chuckled in a faintly pitying way. "Oh, that's what you amateurs are always asking," he replied. "But you have to remember that what we professionals regard as treasure wouldn't turn the head of a member of the general public for a second. There are many different kinds of treasure, dear lady. So now, if you've seen enough, I think I'd better let you get back to whatever it was you were doing, and we'll get back to our work."

"Of course," said Ron. "We'll be out of your hair." He glanced at the other's high forehead. "I mean, so to speak. And thank you for your time."

Tania and Ron backed out of the entrance, removed their shoe covers, and accompanied the professor as he ushered them towards the gate leading to the path back to the farm.

"Thank you so much for that," said Tania, holding out her hand to shake the professor's. "It's been absolutely fascinating. It must be a great responsibility to be in charge of such an important investigation."

The smile on the professor's face seemed to set. "Yes," he replied. "Yes, it is."

"Oh dear." Tania's hand went to her mouth. "Oh, I think I've put my foot in it, haven't I? Because the lady down at the farm said that there was originally someone else in charge, but he died. That's right, isn't it?"

"That is correct, Mrs Faye," responded Edward, tight-lipped. "The original leader of our expedition was Professor Sutherland, but he, as you say, died."

"And it happened here, didn't it? That must have been absolutely ghastly. Does anyone have any idea how it happened?"

"I really couldn't say, Mrs Faye. Obviously the police are investigating, but I'm afraid that I'm not privy to their thinking. I'd prefer to be involved with them as little as possible. In fact, when you arrived and my young colleague called me, I was afraid that you might be the police come to disturb our work once more. But thank goodness, they seem to have left the scene."

"Yes. I can imagine it would be very disruptive having policemen traipsing all over your dig," sympathised Tania. "I'm glad we're not going to be getting in your way any more." She turned to go, before stopping in her tracks. "Oh, there's just one thing. I was right, wasn't I, in saying that you're the head of archaeology at Camford?"

"Yes." The professor's tone was reserved.

"Well then, I wonder why they didn't put you in charge of the dig in the first place. I mean, why would they bring in someone from elsewhere? Unless of course you suggested him yourself."

Edward's nostrils flared. "That's a question you'd need to put to the university authorities," he replied, tight-lipped. "They evidently had their reasons."

"Would it have been that they regarded Professor Sutherland as more experienced than you?" suggested Tania, wide-eyed and artless.

"I really couldn't say," said Edward shortly.

"But I'm sure that wouldn't have affected your work here," said Tania innocently. "I mean, all for the greater good of the project, surely."

"As you say." Edward was not to be drawn.

"I'm sure you're all one big happy family," pressed on Tania. "Tell me, what sort of man was Professor Sutherland?"

"Very well qualified," ground out Edward. "At least, that was the belief of the University authorities."

"So everybody in the team must have respected that, I imagine. Did you know him before? Was he a friendly sort of chap? Did he get on well with everybody?"

Edward was saved from replying by a shout from the entrance to the barrow, where the woman who had appeared from one of the side chambers was standing, pushing a straggle of hair off her face.

"Edward," she called, "I really could do with some help here."

"You'll have to excuse me," said the professor, relief in his voice, and he turned and walked briskly up towards the barrow, disappearing into the interior without a backward glance.

*

Once the couple were safely in the shelter of the other side of the hedge, Ron turned to his wife, bowed, and gave a brief round of applause.

"What on earth was that for?" asked Tania,

amused.

"For giving one of the finest performances of an airhead I have yet to see," grinned Ron. "If I hadn't known better, I'd have begun to wonder what sort of dim-witted woman had inveigled me into marrying her."

"The sort who can ask stupid questions in the hope of worming out some helpful information," smirked Tania in response. "Which I think we managed to do."

"No 'we' about it," asserted Ron. "That was a sterling solo performance. But you're right in saying that we know quite a bit more than we did before. Not least that Professor Wilton here doesn't appear to have been Malcolm Sutherland's greatest fan."

"Of course, there could be a whole lot of reasons for that," mused Tania. "It could be a simple case of jealousy because the other man was put in charge of the expedition over his head. He obviously wasn't too ecstatic about that. Perhaps he didn't think Malcolm was up to the job."

"He did describe him as very well-qualified," pointed out Ron.

"Yes, 'qualified', and he qualified that by describing it as the university authorities' opinion. He didn't actually say that he shared it. But even so, jealousy for whatever reason would be a pretty obvious motive to dislike Malcolm. But motive enough to kill him?" demurred Tania. "Is that going too far?"

"And we don't know how the two got on personally," pointed out Ron. "The professor never got around to answering that question before he was interrupted by that woman up at the barrow. Although it did seem to me that he was slightly relieved to be side-stepping the question, so perhaps there's a conclusion to be drawn from that."

"I think his general manner when the conversation turned to Malcolm told us that already. But who knows whether there were any specific incidents which might have caused the man to boil over? He does seem pretty self-important. Maybe there was some incident which could have made him seethe."

"Such as?"

"Something which prompted him to sneak up on Malcolm at the dig in the middle of the night and do for him with a handy sharp instrument?" suggested Tania, an ironic eyebrow raised. "Really? Come to that, there must have been some reason for Malcolm being there in the first place, and we have no clue as to what that might have been." She sighed. "As ever, more questions than answers."

"Then you will simply have to carry on doing what you are so good at, which is keep talking to people until all the relevant beans have been spilled," proposed Ron. "Don't forget, we've only seen two of the potential people involved so far. There are the other members of the dig team to tackle, like that woman who dragged Professor Wilton away from us, as well as that young ginger-headed boy who was scrabbling about outside the barrow as we passed. Who, by the way, gave us something of a shifty look as we passed before burying his head in whatever it was he was doing. It crossed my mind at the time that it was a little odd. I mean, if a couple of strangers turned up out of the blue where you were working, you'd naturally wonder who they were, wouldn't you?"

"I expect we shall get to them in due course. And there were a couple more that Leah mentioned. They'll be about the place somewhere. Our paths are bound to cross."

"And, I've just thought, there are the others who may have something to tell us. Leah's staff, I mean," observed Ron. "There's the chap who looks after the alpacas. He may have seen or heard something. And don't forget his lady friend, the cleaner woman." He gave a little chuckle. "It could be like one of those Victorian scenarios where people talk in front of the staff because they're invisible, and so they let out all sorts of unguarded information."

"Except that the other side of that coin is the old saying, '*Pas devant les domestiques*'," smiled Tania. "'Not in front of the servants'. Not that I suspect that anyone we've met so far was brought up in a household with servants. But I know what you mean. Eaves-droppings can be wonderful things."

"And, in fact, mention of the cleaning woman - Jane, wasn't it? - reminds me that she also works as a barmaid at the pub in the village. And if the pub is anything like any of the pubs we've been in during your illustrious career as a sleuth, I wouldn't mind betting that it will be a fertile source of information." Ron looked at his watch. "And since breakfast has definitely worn off, and I'm getting a bit of a rumble in my innards, why don't we saunter down to the village pub to see if they can offer us some refreshment? From what little I saw as we came past yesterday, it looks like a pretty traditional country hostelry. At the very least, they ought to be able to do a ploughman's."

"And who knows who we may fall into conversation with when we're there?" agreed Tania. "That, Mr Faye, is an excellent suggestion. I knew I kept you for something."

"Cheek!" responded Ron with a grin. "And for that, Mrs Faye, my first pint is on you. Don't forget to pick up your purse on the way."

The two carried on down the path to the farm, passed through the gate, crossed the farmyard - stopping only at The Byre to collect Tania's handbag under Ron's watchful eye - before setting off down the slightly dusty road, more of a lane, which led to the hamlet of Upson Parva, lying quiet under the midday sunshine.

"I wonder who lives here these days," reflected Ron, as the first of the straggle of cottages came into view. "It's not as if there's much going on around here in the way of employment. I'm guessing in the old days it would have been mostly agricultural workers, but not now."

"I dare say there are still a few working farms around," suggested Tania. "Mind you, if they're anything like Leah's, the number of people employed is probably tiny compared to what it used to be a hundred years ago. But I wouldn't mind betting that most of the tractors you'll find in a village like this nowadays are so-called 'Chelsea tractors' driven by sharp-suited estate agents commuting to Camford or Westchester. Or their trophy wives taking Noah and Jemima to the village school in Upson Major.'

Ron sighed. "Am I an old fogey to mourn the passing of the old days?"

"Of course you are," laughed Tania. "It's one of the reasons I love you."

After passing several cottages, each a reflection of the others with its flower-filled front garden behind a low wall and a brick-and-flint thatched construction variously decked with climbing roses, honeysuckle, or wisteria, the couple reached the Drover's Rest, evidently the chief building of the settlement. The inn consisted of a central structure rising to three storeys, with Georgian sash windows set into a facade of creamy sandstone and a central doorway with a small portico. On either side of the main edifice, which seemed slightly too grand for its setting, ran a muddle of outbuildings, some of which looked like stables surrounding a courtyard reached through an archway, while others sported chimneys which hinted at the existence of on-site brewing. To one side, an extensive car park was dotted with a scatter of cars. Tania and Ron, encouraged by a sign at the roadside which announced 'Lunches, Dinners, and Afternoon Teas - Everything Home-cooked', pushed open the front door and made their way into the main bar.

Chapter 7

"Are we all right to order lunch?" enquired Ron of the man behind the bar who looked up expectantly at their arrival.

"I'd be upset if you didn't," returned the other with a chuckle. He was a burly individual of about sixty, well over six feet in height, with a bush of grizzled hair above a cheerful-looking face set with unusually pale piercing grey eyes. "Was it just a snack you were wanting, or a proper meal?"

"A proper meal, if it's not too much trouble," replied Ron, looking around the almost deserted bar. "I didn't know if you would be serving."

"Mondays is always quiet at lunchtime," said the man. "But we're never so quiet that we can't provide a meal for a hungry traveller. That's what we're here for. Have been for hundreds of years. Ain't going to stop now."

"It's a pretty impressive building," remarked Ron, looking around. "Although I can't help thinking it doesn't quite go with the rest of the cottages in the village. Not exactly vernacular. But you say it's been here for hundreds of years?"

"Ah, not this particular building, it hasn't," replied the man. "The pub is pretty ancient, 'cos it was first established for the drovers, which accounts for its name."

"What exactly is a drover?" wondered Ron. "I thought it might be some sort of misprint for 'driver'."

"Cor! Townies, eh?" chuckled the man. "No, the drovers were the folks who drove the livestock up to London in the old days along the ancient highways. Geese, sheep, all-sorts. Mostly prehistoric routes, they were. And though you wouldn't know it now, but the road up through the village is one of those. Drove roads, they called them. And in fact, you can just about pick it out if you know where to look, but the drove road carries on up the hill and over the Downs until it meets up with the Ridgway up to the north. And the pub first started out in medieval times as a sort of staging post."

"But this building isn't medieval," pointed out Tania.

"Not so much. The cellars are. But the old medieval original burned down in sixteen hundred and something. Timber-framed and thatched, you see. But at the time, this was all part of the de la Mere estate, and the lord at the time decided he didn't want to have to do without the tolls from the pub, so he had the place rebuilt. Story goes that they used the left-over stone from when they were building Mere Hall. Seems his lordship wasn't averse to saving a few quid here and there. So now we have this fine building, and the passing travellers didn't have to go hungry no more."

"Well, I think we qualify as hungry right now," smiled Ron. "Can we take a look at the menu?"

"No such thing in here, sir," responded the man. "But if you'd let me have your order for drinks, and then you can go and take a seat - that table by the window gives you the best view - and then I'll be over to tell you what we've got on offer. By the way, the name's Charlton - William Charlton, owner and licensee of this fine establishment. But everybody round here calls me Billy, so feel free to do the same."

"In that case, Billy, can we please have a G and T for the lady, and I'll have a pint of whatever you recommend as the best local wallop."

"Well, sir, you can't do much better than the stuff we brew ourselves out back, though I says it as shouldn't. So a pint of Drover's Draught it shall be. But you better keep a hold of your socks, 'cos it's pretty strong stuff."

"Thanks for the warning. Oh, and my wife's paying," said Ron.

"Is she indeed?" said Billy, eyebrows raised. "In that case, I'll keep a sharp lookout for her in case she arrives unexpectedly," he chortled. "Sorry, ma'am," he added to Tania. "Sometimes my sense of humour runs away with me. No offence."

"None taken," smiled Tania in response. "And I'm quite used to it from my husband. I'm Tania, by the way - Tania Faye, and this gentleman alongside me, who evidently has no shame in claiming a drink from a lady on account of some imagined slight, is my husband Ron."

"Pleased to meet you," said Billy. "So you sit yourselves down, and I'll be over with your drinks in a jiffy."

Moments later, the drinks delivered, Billy pulled from under his arm a small slate with various items chalked on it. "This is why we don't run to menus," he explained. "On account of all our food is freshly prepared according to what comes in, so the options are always changing. Apart from the Ploughman's, of course, which is always on. Now today we've got a home-made pork and pigeon paté for starters, or else you can have the Wessex Onion soup, which is made with onions from old Jim Wootton's farm down the village, topped with our own farmhouse bread and sprinkled with grated extra-mature Upsondale cheese, which they make down in Upson Major. All local, you see. And then for mains, we got some lovely fresh trout come in this morning - I expect you crossed the trout stream on your way here - and then of course there's the house speciality, rook pie."

"And what goes into that?" enquired Ron.

Billy chuckled. "Why, rooks, of course," he replied, one amused eyebrow raised. "What else?"

"You make a pie out of rooks?" Tania was incredulous.

"Too right we do," grinned Billy. "Good traditional country fare, that is. A bit old-fashioned these days, but none the worse for that. And it's one way of getting some use out of the blighters. You must have seen them perched in all the treetops. Millions of them up around here, there are, cawing away. Sometimes you can't hear yourself think. So every so often, out go my sons Caleb and Joel with their shotguns and bring home a bunch of rooks for the pot. Quite a bit of meat on a rook, there is, and it's all organic. Makes a very tasty pie. So, what'll it be?"

"I think I'll start with the paté, and then go on to the trout," said Tania.

"And I've always been a sucker for a good strong cheese, so it's the soup for me," declared Ron. "And I've never been one to shy away from a challenge, so I'm going to brave your rook pie."

"You won't regret it, sir," smiled Billy confidently. "I'll be away to the kitchen and get that all sorted."

*

"Are you sure I can't tempt you to try this last morsel of pie, love?" enquired Ron as he surveyed the almost empty plate in front of him. "It really is rather good."

Tania repressed a tiny shudder. "You're very kind, but there are limits. I think I'll stick to the more conventional items on the menu."

"Please yourself," retorted Ron, as he cleared the remains of his meal. He looked up as the landlord approached to take away the plates. "You were absolutely right, Billy," he stated. "That pie was an experience. I may never taste its like again. In a good way," he added hastily.

"Kind of you to say so, sir," said Billy. "But I have to say, you're not the first. We do have something of a reputation for our food. Which is why the world pretty much beats a path to our door. Don't be fooled by the fact that we're quiet at the moment. They'll all be descending on us from Westchester and Camford and such, once the evening gets going. So can I ask where you've come from, if you don't mind me being nosy. 'Cos I didn't notice a car."

"Oh, we just walked down from the farm," said Tania. "We're staying there for a few days."

"What, Leah's farm up the way?" queried Billy, eyebrows raised in surprise. "Now that's a turn-up. Because from what I've heard, visitors are suddenly a bit thin at Leah's place, on account of the ..." He hesitated.

"On account of the murder, you mean?" said Tania. "Yes, we know all about that. We're old friends of Leah's. But I'm slightly surprised that the news has found its way to you so quickly."

"Ah, news travels fast in these country villages," replied Billy. "And being as I'm the pub landlord, it tends to get to me quicker than most. Plus, if I'm honest, I've got a bit of an inside source, on account of my barmaid works up at the farm part-time."

"That'll be Jane?" asked Tania, receiving a nod in reply. "I wonder, is she about at the moment? Because we wouldn't mind having a word with her."

"Not around at the moment," said Billy. "Gone off shopping down in Westchester today, being her day off. But she'll be back later."

"In which case," said Tania, "I wonder if you wouldn't mind us picking your brains a little. Since you mention that news tends to come your way."

"That it does."

"And gossip too?" ventured Tania. "Because we may well be in the market for that as well."

"Now this sounds interesting," said Billy.

"Can we get you a drink?" suggested Ron. "And perhaps you can spare a minute to sit down for a little chat."

"Well, I don't see why not," smiled Billy. "Just give me one second. And while I'm about it, what about the same again for you two? On the house." Receiving smiles of acceptance, Billy passed behind the bar and, pushing open a door, shouted through to the kitchen, "Caleb! Come and mind the bar for a minute, would you?" And after the appearance of what was evidently one of his sons, Billy swiftly organised the round of drinks and joined Tania and Ron at their table. "So, what's all this about?"

"The thing is," began Tania, "we're not just staying up at the farm by chance. I'm sure alpacas have their attractions, but they're not what brought us here."

"Go on," said Billy, intrigued.

"We're old friends of Leah's, and she asked us for our help because of what's happened up on the Downs."

"The murder, you mean? But she's not involved, is she? I mean, it didn't take place on her land, did it? And it was one of that history mob from Camford, so what's it to her?"

"Actually," sighed Tania, "in one way she's very much involved. Because the man who died happens to be her ex-husband."

"That tall chap with the white hair? Stone the crows!" exclaimed Billy. "Now how come I never got told that? Wait till I see our Jane. But still, what brings you here? You ain't police or anything, are you?"

"Not at all," said Ron. "But the reason Leah came to us was that Tania's ... well, she's got a bit of experience with murder, one way or another. You see, we live in Ramston, and ..."

"Hang on," interrupted Billy. "Ramston, you say? And murder? That's where they had that business at the abbey a little while back, isn't it? And wasn't there someone called Faye caught up in sorting that out?" He gave Tania a piercing look. "D'you mean to say that was you?"

Tania shrugged in a self-deprecating way, as Ron murmured, "And not just the abbey. Wait till you see this week's news headlines."

"So Leah wants you to help find out who did this killing on her doorstep?"

"It's affecting her livelihood," answered Tania.

"Casting a shadow over her farm and her friends who work there. So of course I said yes. And that's why I think it might be helpful if I had a chat with you. After all, it does sound as if, from what you said, not much goes on around here without you knowing about it."

"I do keep my ear pretty close to the ground," agreed Billy. "So, ask away."

"Would I be right in guessing that the crowd from the dig might come into the pub on occasion?" enquired Tania. "After all, there isn't that much going on around here after working hours, I imagine."

"You'd be right. We are a bit of a social hub here. In fact, you might say that Upson Parva comes up pretty short in terms of vibrant night life, so at least some of them were down here most evenings."

"So I wondered if you had seen or heard anything that might have a bearing on the case. Anything, really. General impressions of people, conversations you might have overheard, that sort of thing."

"I can tell you one thing for starters," said Billy. "It didn't take a lot to work out that that chap in charge ..."

"Malcolm Sutherland," put in Ron

"That'll be the one. Well, he thought a great deal of himself. For a start, you could tell he fancied himself as a ladies' man."

"How so?" asked Tania.

"One night, I was serving at the bar as usual, and I was pulling a pint for someone else, and that woman who works for Leah as her manager, Mary, was stood in front of me, and that Malcolm chap came up behind her and put his arms around her so's she could hardly move. And I heard him say 'Come on, my dear. Why don't you let me buy you a drink?' And she wriggled a bit as if to try to get free, and she said 'No thank you', all sharp like. But he held on and said 'Get a drink or two down you and you'll feel different. Every woman needs a man from time to time', and she managed to get his hands off her, and she hissed at him 'Not if you were the last man on earth! And if you try that again, you'll regret it!'. And she pushed him off and scooted over to her other friends, so I didn't have to put my oar in, which I was just about to do. And I thought, she ought to have given him a good slap." Billy reflected for a second. "And maybe she did. Or worse?"

"We've no reason to think that for the moment," said Tania. "But it sounds as if Malcolm Sutherland was not necessarily the nicest person on the planet."

"Oh, you can say that again," nodded Billy. "Because that's just reminded me of something else I heard another time. See, I was out in the passageway at the back taking a crate of empty bottles out of the way, and it also leads to the gents' toilets. And as I was stood there, that Malcolm fellow came out of the loos, and as he did so he stopped in the doorway and looked back and said 'If you say one word to anybody, you're out! And nobody would believe you anyway. So don't forget, I can make life very difficult for you, boy'. And off he stormed, and a few seconds later that young lad from the dig team, the one with the red hair, he came out of the loo as well. And I never thought anyone with red hair could get any redder, but the lad saw me and blushed scarlet, before he scuttled back into the bar. So I don't know what was going on there, and I probably don't want to guess."

"Maybe Malcolm's interests weren't restricted to just Mary," surmised Ron. "That could make things very awkward."

"I wonder if Leah might have any thoughts on the matter," mused Tania. "We could broach the subject. Delicate, though." She thought for a second. "But coming back to what you first said about Malcolm - that he thought a great deal of himself."

"Oh, that he did," said Billy. "And he wasn't shy about letting other people know why they ought to think a great deal of him too. More than once, I've heard him spouting forth in the bar to anyone who'd listen, and quite a few who'd rather not, about what he'd done and how he'd been called in to oversee this dig because there was nobody else up to the mark. In fact, one time, he dragged one of the village chaps in to prove his point."

"Oh? How do you mean?" asked Ron.

"Well, there's one chap in the village who's mad on history. George Cheverell, it is - lives in one of the cottages just along the way."

"I think Leah mentioned him," said Ron.

"George is our local history buff," continued Billy. "You want to know anything, just ask George. Got his own little museum and everything in his cottage. Haul anyone in to see it, he will. And he volunteered like a shot when they announced that the dig was going to take place. So anyway, there was Malcolm holding forth, and George had just come in for his usual evening pint, and Malcolm dragged him over and said 'The thing is, look at George here. This is one of the reasons they call in the experts, because the local bumpkins like George know nothing. He's fine at scraping about with that old trowel of his, but that's all these people are fit for.' Course, that didn't go down too well with the locals, 'cos George is a good chap and well-liked, and everybody looked the other way and soon drifted off. And I thought, well, maybe it's the drink talking, 'cos he'd had a few, but there was no cause to go embarrassing the fellow like that, so I poured George his pint on the house."

"I almost hate to ask, but I don't suppose there are any other incidents you're aware of?" wondered Tania.

Billy reflected. "Not that I can think of. Oh, hold on. Maybe just one. See, it was closing time, and I was seeing everyone out, and that dig lot were the last out of the door. And I'd noticed that Malcolm had that young girl who's part of the team, young Victoria, he had her cornered at one of the tables and looked to be deep in conversation with her. And she didn't look too happy. No idea what it was about, but as they were passing me in the doorway I just heard him say to her 'If you don't pull up your socks and do exactly what I want from you, there'll be no masters in your future.' Made no sense to me, and then they were gone."

Chapter 8

"You know," reflected Ron as he squinted upwards towards where two or three black dots were circling, to the accompaniment of faint cawing, "I don't think I shall ever look at a rook in quite the same way again." He paused and tried to focus. "I assume those are rooks. Or are they crows?"

"Isn't there an old country saying?" replied Tania, her arm linked in Ron's as the couple set out up the hill to return to the farm. "'A rook on its own is a crow. But a crow in a crowd is a rook'. Or is it the other way round?"

"Thank you, love," laughed Ron. "That's extremely helpful. I shall bear it in mind."

Tania's smiling face grew sober. "And what we also need to be bearing mind is what we've learnt from our conversation with Billy in the pub. There were some interesting revelations, weren't there?"

"You mean in terms of finding out what Malcolm Sutherland was like? That's very true. And Leah had given us virtually nothing in the way of hints about him, other than to say, if I remember correctly, that the charm about him wore off fairly quickly. Maybe we ought to quiz her a bit more about their time together. It might give us a few more insights into him."

"And that other old saying is undoubtedly true," remarked Tania.

"Which is?"

"We've quoted it before. 'Know the man, and you know his murderer'. And I suspect that we're beginning to know rather more about Malcolm, and it doesn't sound as if he was an especially likeable character. I don't know if we've yet got anything that smells like a motive for murder, but we've definitely got some reasons for people to dislike him."

"Mary, for one," said Ron. "Remember, she tensed up when we got on to the subject of Malcolm when we were speaking to her. Didn't seem to want to be forthcoming at all, and then the phone rang, so we couldn't take it any further. But now we have an idea of what she had in mind. If Malcolm was trying it on with her in the pub, virtually in front of other people, he obviously thought that his old irresistible charm was still working."

"Which it evidently was not," observed Tania. "And not that he was exercising that 'charm' when he took it upon himself to embarrass the local chap, George, in front of a pub full of people. That's the sort of arrogance that puts plenty of backs up. And who knows where that might lead?"

"And even though Billy gave him the slight benefit of the doubt, saying that maybe he'd had a drink or two too many and went over the top a bit in his remarks, that doesn't account for what Malcolm was heard to say to the two young people on the team," pointed out Ron. "There's those remarks of Malcolm's to that redhead kid when he was standing in the loo doorway, for a kick-off. Even though, like Billy, I'm not immediately going to put two and two together to make five, there was a definite threat to the boy, whatever the actual situation. And what do they say about red hair? Fiery temper? I know that's a cliché, but the trouble with clichés is that quite often they're true."

"Plus what was said to Victoria when the group was leaving the pub. Not that we've got any inkling as to what was going on, other than that Victoria seemed unhappy about it, but again there was an unmistakeable threat in the way he spoke to her."

"I think it's probably time you brought out your sympathetic agony aunt why-don't-you-cry-on-my-shoulder character, love," suggested Ron with a smile. "I'm sure that'll produce some results."

"I'll give it a try," said Tania. "We'd better head on up."

But before the couple could proceed much further, they were interrupted by a cheery 'Good afternoon' from the direction of the front garden of one of the cottages they were passing. They wheeled, surprised, to see the round smiling face of a middle-aged man, watering-can in hand, standing on the front doorstep of the house.

"Hello," continued the man. "Sorry if I made you jump. Back off up to the farm, are you?"

"Actually, yes, we are," replied Ron.

"Thought as much," said the man, putting down the watering can and advancing down the path to his front gate. "I thought I recognised you."

"Sorry," said Tania, puzzled. "Have we met? Because I don't ..."

"Of course, you haven't the foggiest who I am," laughed the man. "Sorry about that." He held out a hand. "I'm George. George Cheverell. I'm helping out at the dig site up on the Downs."

"Oh. I see. Nice to meet you, George." Tania shook the outstretched hand. "I'm Tania, and this is my husband Ron. But I still don't quite see ..."

"Ah, well, that's it. You couldn't see me, but I could see you," chuckled George. "I was in the barrow this morning when Edward was giving you the guided tour of the workings," he explained, "but of course I was in the dark up at the far end, so you couldn't have seen me."

"Got you," said Ron. "Yes, I remember your team leader did say you were about to start work on the main chamber."

"We are." George's eyes glistened with excitement. "That's to say, I did actually begin on Saturday, but then I was told to stop. Someone else ... well anyway, I'm on it now. And I have to say it's a bit of an honour, so I'm very grateful to Edward for giving me the opportunity, me not being one of the professionals like the others."

"So we gather," smiled Tania. "We've just come from having lunch at the pub, and we got into conversation with the landlord. He was singing your praises as the local history buff. 'You want to know anything' he said, 'just ask George'."

"Oh, that's just Billy's talk," said George, seeming slightly embarrassed. "He's never got a bad word to say about anybody. But ..." He hesitated. "I don't suppose ... seeing as you seem to have a bit of interest in our work ..."

"We do," confirmed Tania. "It was enthralling, what your colleague was telling us this morning." She regarded George quizzically.

"Well, I wondered if you'd like to take a look at my own little museum inside," ventured George diffidently. "Actually, calling it a museum's a bit grand. It's just a bit of a display. You see, I've had this thing about history ever since I was a boy, and I've been on a few digs and done a bit of detectoring on my own, so I've got a few finds in a cabinet. Some of them are quite interesting. But I wouldn't want to impose ..."

Ron and Tania exchanged a look. "No, actually, that would be fascinating," said Ron. "We come from Ramston, and my wife's always been interested in the town's history, so we'd love to see your collection."

"In you come, then," smiled George, pushing open the front door and leading the way into the sitting room, cosily furnished with large squashy armchairs in front of a brick inglenook fireplace, and with the opposite wall taken up by a glass-fronted cabinet whose shelves were full of a miscellany of objects.

"Goodness, that is quite a collection!" exclaimed Tania. "You must have started when you were a boy."

"I did," said George. "In fact ..." He scanned the shelves. "There," he pointed. "That was my very first find."

Ron peered more closely at the indicated object and frowned. "I'm afraid you'll have to explain it to me. I'm not up on these things. All I can see is a little lump of ... is that silver?"

"It is," responded George, his enthusiasm in no way dimmed. "That," he declared, "is a *sceat*."

"A what?" queried Ron. "A shat?"

"Sorry, doesn't sound very nice," admitted George. "Or more politely known as a *sceatta*. It's a very early form of penny. I found it when I was very young, on holiday with my parents. We'd gone down to Hengistbury Head ..."

"Near Bournemouth?" said Tania. "I know it."

"And I was playing on my own among some bushes, and there were rabbit burrows there, and I saw this thing shining in the sandy soil, so I dug it out, picked it up and went to show my dad. He cleaned it up, and it turned out to be a little silver coin. Of course, we didn't have any such thing as the internet to look things up, so when we got home we went to the library and discovered that it was a very early penny. They were minted by the Anglo-Saxons and the Jutes in the seven-hundreds, just when they were invading England. I suppose it had been dropped there and buried, and the rabbits had somehow brought it to the surface when they were digging out their burrows. And if you look closely you can just make out the profile of a man wearing some sort of a crown."

Tania put her head closely to the case. "Oh yes. I see. How interesting."

"And in fact, the legends do say that some of the invasions were led by a pair of warrior brothers called Hengist and Horsa, which is how Hengistbury Head got its name. So I like to think that my little coin actually carries a portrait of Hengist himself. Probably nonsense," confessed George diffidently, "but it's my little conceit."

"Shouldn't you have handed it in to the authorities at the time?" wondered Ron. "Aren't there rules about these things?"

"Oh, there are," agreed George. "And I wouldn't dream of not doing so these days. Whatever might turn up." There was a gleam in his eye. "But I was so young, and so proud of what I'd found, that we didn't say anything. And after all, where was the harm if nobody else knew about it?"

"None at all, really," agreed Tania. She pointed and frowned. "What's that? It doesn't look very historic."

"What?" George looked momentarily concerned, but then his face cleared. "Oh, that's just my old trowel. It's what I used to use when I started, years ago. It's a bit battered now. I started to use it at the barrow, but I don't any more."

"It does look a bit fragile," remarked Tania, observing the crumbling state of the wooden handle. "The rest of it's still lovely and shiny, though. So what other things are you particularly proud of?"

"No other precious metals, I'm afraid," said George. "There's a lead pilgrim badge from the shrine of Thomas Becket there, which I found one day up on the Ridgway. It must have come loose from the hat of some traveller who'd visited the saint's tomb in Canterbury Cathedral. I dare say he would have been very put out that he couldn't show it to all his family and friends when he got back home. These things were quite literally a badge of faith."

"I've seen scallop shells from the shrine at Santiago de Compostella," remarked Tania. "They were the first tourist souvenirs, weren't they?" She scanned the case. "What else should I be looking at?"

"That key's quite interesting. I don't know if you know, but they suspect that there's a Roman villa somewhere under one of the farms just outside Westchester. Nobody's found it yet, although there are quite a few pieces of roof tile scattered across some of the fields there. And I was walking along a footpath around the edge of one of those fields one day, with my metal detector, and I got a bleep. I thought it was probably just a bottle-top - it usually is - but there it was, just under the surface. A Roman key made of iron, for a little box or chest. Too small to be for a house, so they'll just have to keep searching for that villa."

"And it looks so ordinary," observed Ron. "It could easily be quite modern."

"I assure you, it isn't," retorted George with a hint of sharpness. "I wouldn't make a mistake like that."

"I'm sure you wouldn't," said Tania. "So, one last thing, and then we really ought to be on our way."

"What about that little flask?" offered George. "Tudor green glaze, and virtually intact apart from one tiny chip on the rim. I have a feeling it was made for perfume or some precious oil. That came out of a midden they unearthed when they were digging the foundations for a petrol station on the Westchester bypass."

"It's very pretty," smiled Tania. "And now we mustn't take up any more of your time. I'm sure you must have things to do."

George took a guilty glance at his watch. "You're absolutely right. In fact, I shouldn't be here at all. I only popped down from the dig during my lunch break to give my plant pots a drink. They dry out so quickly, but I really must get back, or I shall be in hot water, sorry, no pun intended, from the boss."

"That's the new boss, isn't it?" said Ron. "The chap who showed us around this morning."

"Edward? That's right," nodded George.

"He seems a very pleasant chap. How has he settled into his new responsibility? Because we heard about the sudden change up there."

"That's one way of putting it," replied George drily.

"And all so very unfortunate," said Tania. "I mean, what a shocking thing to happen. A murder, and you all such a closely-knit team, or so I assume."

"Of course," said George, with a bright smile.

"Because I can easily imagine that, with a group of professionals working in such close proximity, there could easily be tensions."

"I wouldn't know about that. After all, I'm not a professional."

"Oh goodness," said Tania, hand to her mouth. "Sorry, I didn't mean to offend you."

"Not at all," responded George. "No, I'm just an enthusiastic amateur. And I was very lucky to be accepted when I volunteered to take part in the dig. It's a great privilege."

"You must have been very grateful to the leader - the former leader, I mean. I expect he was glad to welcome you." A small silence fell. "Nice chap, was he?" continued Tania, determined to obtain some sort of reaction.

"We all had our responsibilities," said George with a hint of evasion. "We pretty much stuck to those. There isn't a great deal of socialising going on when you're on your hands and knees scraping away layers."

"So you wouldn't have been aware of any tensions in the group?" persisted Tania. "No clashes? No reasons for anyone to dislike the man in charge? Or to wish him harm?"

"I suppose he might have had a bit of a downer on the two young students," replied George. He seemed reluctant to go into any detail. "But as I say, we were all busy concentrating on our own jobs." He looked at his watch again. "Speaking of which, I really must get back, or Edward will be wondering where on earth I've got to. I don't want him putting me on sieving duty of the spoil heap as a punishment. I'll see you out."

Almost before they knew it, Tania and Ron were back on the roadside, watching the rapidly diminishing figure of George Cheverell as he hurried up the hill towards the farm.

*

"There's someone else who's reluctant to give Malcolm Sutherland a glowing character reference," observed Ron, as he and Tania resumed their leisurely stroll up the hill. "It does begin to build a picture, doesn't it?"

"Put that together with what Billy told us about that incident in the pub," replied Tania, "and, not to put too fine a point on it, George was lying, or as near as dammit. Or at the very least, evading the question. And I know there's the convention of not wanting to speak ill of the dead, but there is also such a thing as being too tight-lipped."

"I suppose it's one disadvantage of us being totally unofficial. I mean, the police can ask penetrating questions, and if they get a sense that you're concealing something from them, then they're going to badger you until they worm it out of you."

"Mixed metaphors notwithstanding." Tania smiled fondly at her husband.

"Although," continued Ron, "George did go so far as to mention that Malcolm didn't seem to be too fond of the two younger members of the dig team, for whatever reason."

"And again, that chimes with what Billy told us about the remarks he overheard in the pub. Irrespective of whatever the reasons might have been, that all sounded like bullying to me."

"But he still didn't give us any indication of any animosities going in the other direction. We'll need to continue our programme of harmless chats with them and see what comes out of it," said Ron. "But coming back to George, I'll tell you one thing that struck me, and that's his absolute love of his subject and his commitment to the dig. Even though Malcolm was so plainly dismissive of him, it doesn't seem to have put him off. And that little museum of his was really quite impressive in its own small way. Couldn't you just feel his thrill when he found each of the objects in that case?"

"I could," agreed Tania. "An amateur in the true original sense of the word." She drew a breath. "Is this hill getting longer, or is it just me?"

"Old age creeping up on you, love?" chuckled Ron. "Don't worry. We're almost there, and if all else fails I can always give you a choogy-back the rest of the way."

"A what?" enquired Tania, perplexed.

Ron laughed. "If I may quote Billy the landlord, 'Townies, eh?' A choogy-back is what we country folk call what you urbanites would call a piggy-back."

"And when did you become a local yokel?" enquired Tania with a smile.

"It's the rural surroundings," replied Ron. "They're obviously having an effect."

"The only effect I want at the moment is a nice cup of tea with my feet up," retorted Tania.

"And perhaps a proper siesta? With the curtains closed, and your loving husband in attendance?" suggested Ron, one roguish eyebrow raised.

Tania slapped him playfully. "Tea first," she insisted. "And then," she dimpled, "we'll see."

Chapter 9

"Your wake-up tea, madam."

Tania, in the dim light of the curtained bedroom, stretched luxuriously. "My third cup of tea in bed in one day? I must have been a very good girl." Her eyes twinkled as she regarded her husband.

"And nothing is too good for my beloved wife," replied Ron with an answering smile. "And isn't there a rhyme about a good little girl who was very, very good, but when she was bad, she was terrific?" He ducked as Tania threw a pillow at him. "However, this is designed to wake you up and kick-start the little grey cells. Don't forget, we're on a mission, and time's a-wasting. There's suspects to interview, you know."

"You make it sound so formal," said Tania, struggling into a sitting position. "Remember, all I'm doing is engaging in harmless casual conversation with people. And if I happen to learn something useful in the process, that's a bonus."

"Yes, dear," grinned Ron. "And you've caught me like that many a time. I long ago gave up trying to keep my plans for your birthday a secret. Whereas this is all rather more serious than figuring out my choice of present."

"You're right," agreed Tania. "So, let me have my tea and a quick freshen-up, and we'll get back on the hunt for the truth. Any suggestions as to where we start?"

"How about we pick up on what George Cheverell mentioned when he said that Malcolm wasn't exactly the nicest person when it came to the two young people involved in the dig?"

Tania searched her memory. "That's Victoria and Stephen, isn't it? Good plan." She swung her legs out of bed and took a swift gulp of tea. "Right. Give me a few minutes to get myself sorted out, and then we'll go off in search of one or other of them."

"Your wish in my command, love," said Ron, and closed the bedroom door behind him.

*

As the pair emerged from The Byre, they were just in time to see the figure of a young woman entering one of the other buildings fronting on to the farmyard.

"There's a happy coincidence," remarked Ron. "There goes Victoria, so I think our choice is made." The couple followed the figure into the grass-scented interior of the lofty beamed barn.

"Good afternoon," trilled Tania, causing the young woman to turn in surprise. "Sorry - I didn't mean to make you jump. I hope we're not disturbing you."

"Er ... no. That's fine."

"Victoria, isn't it? You're part of the dig team, aren't you?"

"That's right." A shy smile. "Victoria Whaddon. Were you wanting something?"

"Only a little look round, if that's all right with you," replied Tania. "I'm Tania, and this is my husband Ron. We're staying at the farm, and we were lucky enough to be shown around the dig this morning by the man in charge. He told us all about your work, and said that the things you'd found were laid out in the barn down here, so we just wondered if we could have a peep."

"Oh, that's you, is it?" said Victoria. "Edward did say at lunchtime that he'd had some visitors this morning." She pulled a face. "Actually, more than one set of visitors. But I think you were a little more welcome than the police."

"Of course," said Tania, a look of sympathy on her face. "You've had that awful tragedy up there, haven't you? Such a terrible thing to happen."

"Yes," said Victoria, her features displaying no emotion. "But Edward says we have a job to do, and we mustn't let anything get in the way of our work. We have to carry on like professionals, so that's what we're doing."

"I think that's admirable," remarked Ron. "So exactly where do you fit into the team?"

"I'm the osteo-archaeologist," said Victoria, sounding a little more self-assured. "Or," she added, in response to Ron's puzzled frown, "if you want the simpler version, the bones person."

"You've found bones?" enquired Ron, intrigued.

"Five sets, actually." Victoria gestured to two long tables covered with plastic sheeting. "They're laid out there at the moment, before we send them back to the university for detailed scientific examination. I can show you if you like, but please don't touch anything."

"I don't think there's much chance of my fiddling about with old bones," muttered Ron in an aside to Tania, as the couple followed Victoria over to where the tables stood. "Wow!" he exclaimed, as Victoria carefully drew back the coverings. "That is quite a lot of bones."

"We have been very lucky," smiled Victoria. "Sometimes skeletal remains are badly degraded, depending on the nature of the soil they're buried in, but these skeletons are quite surprisingly well-preserved."

"What causes them to be degraded?" wondered Tania.

"Oh gosh," laughed Victoria. "That needs either a two-hour lecture or an answer that's so basic it's pretty meaningless."

"Let's go for basic and meaningless," chuckled Ron.

"In which case, it's very often down to the pH of the adjacent material."

"Acid or alkaline?" said Tania.

"In a couple of words, yes."

"That's good enough for me," said Ron. "You seem to have quite a few people. And that skull there – I swear that chap's looking at me. If it is a chap," he added.

"It is. And I think that's my favourite of all of them," replied Victoria, with a mixture of fondness and pride. "He was the first to emerge when we began work. He was a young man in his early prime, and there are indications that he might have been a warrior."

"Why do you say that?" asked Tania.

"Because of what was found with him. It was quite exciting, actually. Edward believes it to be a bronze torc ..."

"A what?" enquired Ron.

"A neck collar. The finest ones were made of gold – lots of strands twisted together, usually. Worn by civilisations from the Persians to the Vikings, so Edward says, and given to acknowledge bravery. They were designed never to be taken off. It's gone to Camford for analysis. Our young man must have been important. And I know we're supposed to regard them impersonally," she confessed, "but in my mind I like to call him Beowulf."

"After the hero in the Anglo-Saxon poem," observed Tania.

Victoria blushed. "That's right. I know it's silly, but sometimes people forget that skeletons were once people with thoughts and emotions."

"I don't think it's silly at all," declared Ron. "It sounds quite respectful to me." He scanned the rest of the display. "So who else have you got?"

"Actually," said Victoria, "this next group may have something of a tragic tale associated with them. It's a young woman, buried together with two little children."

"Is that what those tiny bones are?" enquired Tania, looking more closely. "So would that be a mother and babies? And why would they be together? Do you have any idea how they died?""

"We simply don't know," answered Victoria. "There's nothing so far to indicate any details. But perhaps the lab may turn up something."

"How sad," mused Tania. "And there's this last one."

"Who I like to think of as 'grandmother'. It's an elderly woman, and she had some grave goods with her which might mean that she was of some status."

"Why are the bones in that crouched position?" wondered Ron. "All the others are laid out straight. What makes this one different?"

"That's something else we don't yet know," replied Victoria. "Everything is laid out as we found it. These remains were in a grave-cut in the floor of the chamber. It may be that the foetal position, which is what we call it, is in some way related to the woman's age, being more common with earlier burials. Something else to which we're still looking for the answer."

"And didn't your Mr Wilton say that you're hoping that there are more finds to come when you get around to excavating the end chamber of the barrow?" asked Tania. "We happened to run into your Mr Cheverell on our way back from the pub at lunchtime, and he says that you're about to carry on with the next section. Such a relief, I imagine. Because the business with the former leader of your team must have thrown you all into a state of complete uncertainty."

"It did rather," responded Victoria. Her former enthusiasm disappeared instantly, to be replaced by a more reserved tone.

"I say 'business', but in fact I'm pussy-footing around the subject," said Tania. "There you all are, excavating sets of historical human remains, and all of a sudden you're presented with a dead body that's all too modern. Because it's a plain case of murder, isn't it? And you have to wonder why on earth somebody would want to kill such an eminent academic as Professor Sutherland. Because I gather that that's what he was."

"So they told us," said Victoria.

"Of course," continued Tania, "because from what

I understand, he was brought in over the head of your own Professor of Archaeology at the university. That's Mr Wilton, isn't it? So he would be your actual head of department, I'm guessing. In charge of assessing your work here and on your course?"

"That's right," agreed Victoria.

"I expect it caused a few eyebrows to rise when Professor Sutherland was brought in over his head," said Tania. "Tell me, did it cause any ill-feeling at the time?"

"I really couldn't say," shrugged Victoria. "These decisions were made by people high up in the admin. None of us in the department had any sort of say."

"And how did you find Professor Sutherland, once you got to know him? Was he easy to work with?"

Victoria hesitated. "He did have some pretty high standards," she replied eventually, "but we were told that he was extremely experienced, so maybe that was only to be expected."

"And was he a nice man, over and above all that?" persisted Tania. "Did you get on well with him personally? Did you like him?"

Victoria gave a slightly tight smile. "It wasn't really up to any of us to like him or not. He was just the man in charge, so he directed operations."

"And ... how do I put this delicately?" said Tania. "Did he like you? That's to say, did he ever overstep the mark in terms of friendliness? I'm sure you understand what I'm getting at."

"Me?" scoffed Victoria. "I think that's one thing I can say wasn't a problem. I never had that sort of issue with him. Far from it. If you think he was getting too familiar with me, or however you want to put it, you're wide of the mark."

"So there weren't any personality clashes along the way? With you or anyone else? Nobody would have had any reason to dislike the professor, or to wish him harm in any way? To your knowledge, of course."

"As you say," said Victoria. "To my knowledge." She seemed increasingly uneasy at the barrage of questioning. "Look, if you don't mind, I really ought to be getting on with my work." She reached for a pair of flimsy rubber gloves. "I hate these," she remarked. "They make my hands all clammy. But Professor Sutherland insisted that we wear them when handling the finds. Something to do with not contaminating them with our DNA."

"We'll let you get on then," said Ron. "We didn't mean to distract you. But thank you for your time. It's been absolutely fascinating. Tania, shall we make a move? Do you fancy a cup of tea?"

"Certainly," nodded Tania. "And thank you again, Victoria." She and Ron made their way out of the hay-barn and back into the central courtyard of the farm.

*

"I will confess to being somewhat confused," admitted Ron, seated in the kitchen of The Byre, a steaming mug of tea in front of him.

"How so?" enquired Tania.

"Well, yet again we've got some contradictory information. Clearly, it seems that none of the dig people are going to utter a syllable of criticism about Malcolm Sutherland. At least, so far. Perhaps if we dig a little deeper, no pun intended, there may be some cracks in that facade. But there's Victoria, saying she had no issues personality-wise with Malcolm, whereas according to Billy Charlton, the man was overheard uttering words of a very unfriendly nature to her. What exactly was the nature of that threat? And she said that there was no hint of Malcolm making any sort of unwelcome advances to her - 'far from it', she said - while we know that he was very willing to push his luck in that department with Mary Winterbourne, as attested by Billy Charlton. The other side of the coin being that other situation in the pub with Stephen Tisbury. All right, we may all be putting two and two together to make twenty-two, but it's not beyond the bounds of possibility that there may have been some sort of ... approach from Malcolm, shall we say, which backfired. Or have we completely misunderstood?"

"Perhaps when we get around to speaking to Stephen, that will all become a little clearer," replied Tania. "But as far as Victoria goes, I'm having trouble imagining what Malcolm might have had against her. She seems very efficient, and dedicated to her work, to judge by the way she was speaking when she was explaining the finds from the excavation. But she's certainly hiding something from us. Whether it's something which Malcolm said or did to her, over and above that incident in the pub, we don't know. But whatever it may have been, whether there was some sort of threat to her personally, or to her future standing at the university, there could be a motive for her to wish him harm, however flimsy that might be."

"No point in drawing any premature conclusions as yet," observed Ron. "We've still got a couple of the dig team to speak to. We may be able to get some clarification from young Stephen of the ginger hair, plus there's Anne something-or-other, whom we haven't clapped eyes on yet."

"Actually, we have," Tania corrected him, "although not in any meaningful sense. Don't you recall, she appeared in the gloom at the far end of the barrow when we were getting our guided tour, and then she stuck her head out to call Edward Wilton away."

"Yes, and just as you looked as if you might be getting some helpful answers from him," observed Ron. "She appears to be rather more mature than some of the others. Didn't Leah describe her as something of a mother hen to the team? Maybe we'll get some better and straighter answers out of her."

"Don't hold your breath," remarked Tania. "Not if

everything that's happened so far is anything to go by. And I'm going to include Leah in that. She certainly hasn't spilled all the beans as far as her history with Malcolm is concerned, and I'd dearly love to know why."

"You don't actually think that she might have had a hand in what happened to him, do you?" asked Ron, amazed.

"No, of course not," replied Tania. "She's got a rock-solid alibi, which is probably just as well for her, if the police get a sniff of any skeletons in her past with Malcolm. But I need to know what those skeletons are if I'm going to have any chance of helping her by working out what did happen here on Saturday night."

"Well then," said Ron, downing the last of his tea. "No time like the present. Let's go and see her, so that we can add a few more skeletons to the ones we've already seen today."

*

When Leah answered the farmhouse door, a look of relief appeared on her face when she realised who her visitors were. "Oh, it's you," she said, with a sigh.

"Charming," said Ron. "We might have hoped for a slightly warmer welcome than that."

"Sorry," replied Leah, beckoning them in and gesturing towards the sofa in the sitting room. "Only I've had the police here this lunchtime, and I was afraid they were back again with more questions."

"No," said Tania. "Actually, it's me, with more questions of my own. I have a feeling that there may be quite a bit of background as regards Malcolm which you haven't mentioned. And if the conversations I've had with some of the team and the locals are anything to go by, I suspect your history with him may not have been quite as simple as you indicated."

Leah gave a deep sigh. "You're not wrong. In fact, you could probably describe our time together as brief but interesting."

"As in, 'May you live in interesting times'?" queried Ron.

Leah gave a wry smile. "Correct." She rose, crossed to a decanter on a side table, poured herself what looked like a substantial measure of whisky, and sat back down. "So, Tania, ask your questions."

"We've learnt quite a lot about Malcolm's character," began Tania, "and it sounds as if the charm you mentioned was somewhat superficial. Not to put too fine a point on it, he sounds to have been something of a bully."

"Never to me," responded Leah swiftly. "And I take it to mean that you're speaking verbally rather than physically. Because I've never heard of him raising so much as a finger to anybody while we were together."

"Verbally, certainly," nodded Tania.

"It may all depend on how you characterise bullying. These days, if you so much as criticise somebody's work style, or even just laugh at them for doing something stupid, you're accused of being a bully. I'd say that Malcolm had very high professional standards, and he probably voiced them strongly. But I can see that somebody might take against him for that."

"There is something else we've learnt about him which might have surfaced during your marriage." Tania hesitated as if wondering how best to approach the subject. "It seems as if Malcolm may have made … overtures of a personal nature, shall we say, to more than one of the dig team. I wonder what your thoughts might be on that?"

Leah let out a surprisingly generous laugh. "No news there, my dear. To put it bluntly, he had the morals of an alley-cat."

Ron's eyebrows rose in astonishment. "You knew that?"

"I knew it, and I discounted it. In fact, when we met, it was pretty well-known that he had a string of relationships on the go. And he wasn't too choosy – 'anything with a pulse' seemed to be his mantra. It was best not to ask too many questions. But I took one look and decided I was going to get him, and I did. To the exclusion of all others, I might add. I made sure of that. Well, for a time, anyway, but it turned out the leopard couldn't change its spots, so we eventually went our separate ways. And it sounds, without asking you for any names from his dig team, as if Malcolm had reverted to his old habits. Which I could easily understand could lead to a 'hell hath no fury' scenario."

"We're ruling nothing out," said Tania. "And are the police aware of all this? You said they'd come asking questions."

"I gave them the broad picture," said Leah, smiling grimly. "It's up to them what they do with it. But I doubt if we've seen the last of them. That Inspector Copper seems pretty tenacious."

"That he is," agreed Ron. "But nowhere near as Tania when she's got her teeth into a situation."

"So what's your plan, now that you're armed with these extra revelations?" asked Leah.

"Simply carry on asking questions," replied Tania. "We've spoken to most of the expedition people so far, with a couple still to go, and of course there are some of your staff members to see."

Leah thought for a moment. "Here's a suggestion. Your cover story is that you've come up here to spend a few relaxing days with the alpacas, so why don't you do just that? I'll have a word with Henry, my chap who mainly looks after them, and we'll arrange for him to take you on an alpaca walk down the valley in the morning. That'll give you an ideal opportunity for a chat with him and find out anything helpful he may know."

"Brilliant plan," smiled Ron. "Come on, Tania love. Time to give our walking boots a polish."

Chapter 10

The knock at the door of The Byre came sharp at nine o'clock the following morning. Tania answered, to find a tweed-clad grizzled middle-aged individual of medium height with a bushy full beard, diffidently twisting his flat cap in his hands, looking up at her from the doorstep.

"Good day, ma'am," he greeted her. "Leah tells me you're wanting to go for a walk with our beasts this morning."

"Well, that's why we're here," returned Tania brightly. "And you're Henry, I assume."

"That's right, ma'am," replied the man. "Henry Gifford. I look after all the animals here, and I organise all the walks."

"Goodness, that's a responsibility," said Tania. "And the picnics too? Because you offer those as well, don't you?"

"We know they do, love," said Ron, coming to his wife's side. "We came here some time ago with some friends for a picnic, Henry, and one of your alpacas pinched my cake."

"And as you can see, he still hasn't got over the trauma," laughed Tania.

"Sorry about that, sir. But I'm afraid that some of the animals have got a bit of a sweet tooth. We try not to let them get within reach of the visitors' food, but they can be pretty crafty at times. But I'm not always about for the picnics. That's our Mary's job," said Henry. "She's better on the customer relations side of things, sir."

"And don't worry too much about the 'sir' and 'ma'am'," advised Ron. "If you're Henry, then I'm Ron, and my wife is Tania."

"Right you are, sir." Henry gave a bashful smile. "Sorry, sir – old habits die hard. So, if you're ready, shall we make a start? It's a beautiful morning and the ground's dry, so you won't need coats or wellies."

"Where are you taking us?" enquired Tania.

"That depends on how far you want to go," said Henry.

"We're fairly fit," said Ron, "so can we make it a good long walk? That'll give us a good appetite for lunch. We'll leave it up to you."

"Right you are, sir. In that case, we'd better go and sort out your beasts." Henry led the way through the gate in the corner of the farmyard and headed for the paddocks.

"By the look of it," remarked Ron, scanning the fields, "you seem to have more than one kind of animal here."

"Oh, they're all alpacas," replied Henry. "Just different sorts. But we don't have any other of their South American relatives here. Too much trouble, in my experience."

"Why's that?" wondered Tania.

"Well, for a start, llamas have got some pretty disgusting personal habits. They'll spit at you soon as look at you, and the big ones can have a pretty long range. Not exactly customer-friendly. But they're good beasts of burden. Now vicuñas, they're a different matter. They fancy themselves something terrible. It's like coping with the Real Housewives of Peru. Beautiful coats, though. No, alpacas have the best temperament for what we do."

"You're very knowledgeable on the subject," said Tania.

"I should be. I worked in the camel house at a zoo down in the West Country for years. But when I came here to help Leah settle her first animals in, suddenly this place felt like home, so I never left."

"So what are the different sorts of alpacas?" enquired Ron.

"We've got Suris and Huacayas. The Suris are the

stockier ones you can see over there. We keep them mostly for the fleece, which fetches a better price, but it's a bit greasy, so not too good for snuggling up to by kids on walks. We don't want mothers complaining. Not again." Henry grinned ruefully. "Most of our animals are Huacayas. Like these here." He chirruped, and a small group of lighter-built alpacas trotted over. "Can't fault them for friendliness. So, pick your animal."

"Can we have one each?" asked Tania.

"Don't see why not," said Henry.

"I like the white one," said Tania. "She's got lovely eyes."

"Lima, eh? Good choice, ma'am. How about you, sir ... I mean, Ron?"

"I quite like the look of the brown one. He's got a bit of a swagger to him."

"Santiago, you mean? Yes, he's a bit of a handful sometimes, but he's good-natured. Right, let me get a couple of halters for them, and we'll be on our way. Give me two seconds." Henry trotted back down the path to the farm, returning swiftly with two halters which he expertly fitted on to the two alpacas. "And here," he said, handing over a small packet to each of the visitors. "Stick those in your pocket. It's just a little bag of pony nuts, in case our friends should need a little encouragement at any point."

"Maybe I should have come armed with some cake," quipped Ron.

"Come along then, you two," said Henry to the alpacas as he opened the gate to let them through. "No, not you lot!" he exclaimed to the rest of the animals who seemed eager to join the expedition. "Next time, maybe." He turned to Tania and Ron. "Right. Hold the halters so that there's about a foot or two of slack between your hand and the animal's mouth. That's it. Now they'll come along with you quite happily. And off we go." He led the way back down the path, across the farmyard, and on to the road down towards the village.

"Where are we going?" asked Tania.

"I thought you might like my favourite walk. It goes down through the woods at the back of the village and along the stream there, almost as far as Upson Major, and then we swing back and come up across some farmland. You might see some wildlife. We've even got a family of great bustards living up on the downs."

"We're in your hands." Ron smiled contentedly as Santiago fell into step alongside him, with Tania and Lima a few paces behind.

"And this is where we go off-road," announced Henry, as he turned into a grassy path at the side of a cottage, leading towards the trees behind it. "There's a chalk stream rises just above here, so we'll follow it down through the valley. You might even see some trout."

"Isn't this George Cheverell's cottage?" enquired Tania.

"You know George?"

"We met him on our way back from lunch at the pub yesterday," explained Tania. "In fact, he invited us in to see his little collection of treasures."

Henry chuckled. "Oh, that's George. Our local historian. I think everyone's been dragged in to see his display at some time or another. He's a little bit obsessed, but he's a good sort. Loves these beasts too, he does," he added, patting Santiago's neck. "Always finds a little treat for them if he's in his garden when we pass, or else when he pops up to the farm just to say hello to them. And he was like a dog with two tails when he got the chance to work on the excavation." He frowned slightly. "A bit of a shame, really."

"Why do you say that?" asked Tania, her instincts alerted.

"Well, it would have been nice if he'd been appreciated a bit more," said Henry. "I mean that chap in charge ..."

"Malcolm Sutherland, you mean? The one who's been killed?"

"The very man. Now I don't say he deserved it, because that's going too far, but he certainly had no cause to speak to George the way he did."

"Why? What did he say?"

"I was in the yard – I'd just been checking with Mary about the dates we'd booked for the shearers next spring – and I came out of the Tack Room just as George came through the gate from the dig. And the Sutherland chap was coming out of the hay-barn, where they've put all their finds, and George went up to him and said 'Malcolm, look at this. It's just come out of the ground up there, so I've brought it to add to the finds down here'. And Sutherland took one look at it and said 'Can you really not tell a rabbit bone from a human? God, sometimes you're just a - forgive my French, ma'am - a useless amateur prat. Wouldn't it be nice if, just once, you could show me some work that's got some value?'. And he stormed off up towards the dig, and George carried on into the barn. He looked pretty crest-fallen."

"Not behaviour guaranteed to endear Malcolm to his team-member," mused Ron.

"You'd not say Sutherland had the most endearing personality all round," remarked Henry.

"Why, did you by any chance hear him say anything of the sort to anyone else?" asked Tania.

"I did," replied Henry. "More than one person, as it happens."

"Such as who?"

"He didn't seem to have a good word for any of the people who were working for him. No matter who they were. Great or small."

"You mean ..."

Henry turned to Tania. "Are you sure you want to hear all this, ma'am?" he asked, a troubled look on his face. "I mean, it's pretty much tittle-tattle, and I can't see how me telling tales on a man who's dead is going to do any good."

"And that's where you're wrong," insisted Tania. "I dare say you care about Leah? She's a good employer?" A nod from Henry. "Well, she's worried about the effect that Malcolm's death is having on the business, and in fact on all of you, staff or dig team. She needs to know what happened, not only for her own peace of mind, but for everyone else's. And to let you into a confidence, that's why she's asked us if we can find out anything helpful which might point towards a solution. So knowing how things stood between Malcolm and other people is an important part of that. Do you see?"

Henry scratched his beard and stood in thought for several long seconds, before finally giving a decisive nod. "You're right, ma'am. But ... if it's all the same to you, could we walk and talk at the same time. After all, I'm meant to be doing my job, taking you for a relaxing walk with these two." He gestured towards the alpacas, who had been standing patiently but were now showing signs of restlessness. "Otherwise the beasts will be starting to complain."

"Of course," smiled Tania. "Let's carry on, and we'll see if we can't multi-task."

The group resumed their walk, entering the belt of woodland that ran downhill behind Upson Parva's straggle of cottages, and following the course of a path that ran alongside the small stream in its centre.

"So you were about to mention words that passed between Malcolm and some other members of his team," Tania reminded their guide.

"Oh, not just some," responded Henry. "All. Starting at the top."

"What, Mr Wilton?" queried Ron. "I would have thought that, being a university professor of archaeology, he'd have been entitled to some respect."

"Not if you'd heard Sutherland speaking to him. You see, I was up in the top paddock one afternoon. It had been quite a hot day, so I was making sure that the animals' drinking trough was filled up. Now the trough in the top paddock is quite near the boundary hedge, which grows quite tall there, and I could hear voices coming from the other side of the hedge, although I couldn't see the people. And the thing is, they couldn't see me."

"And so you could overhear the conversation, even though you may well not have wished to," said Tania with an understanding smile. "But you could hear who it was? And what was said?"

"You couldn't mistake that Scottish accent of Sutherland's," replied Henry. "And what I want to know is, how come he sounded like a glede under a door when he spoke, when Leah herself is so gently-spoken."

"Hmmm. You've never been directed by her in a play," muttered Ron under his breath. "So," he continued aloud, "he was speaking to …?"

"Professor Wilton. At least, it must have been, because I'd recognise George's voice, and it wasn't him, and that ginger-haired boy's voice would have been just too young."

"So what was said?" asked Tania

"You talked about respect," said Henry. "Well, there wasn't much of that in evidence just then. In fact, Sutherland said how amazed he'd been when he heard that Mr Wilton had been made head of the department at Camford. He'd heard about his work, he said, and none of it was anything to write home about. He said that, instead of being promoted, Mr Wilton should have been put out to grass years ago. Anybody would have been better in his job than him."

"Wow! That can't have gone down too well," remarked Ron. "How did Mr Wilton react?"

"That's the thing," said Henry. "He didn't. It all went quiet, and then Sutherland called out 'Nothing to say? No surprise there', so I assume Mr Wilton had just walked off and left him."

"How did these people put up with working under these conditions?" wondered Tania. "It can't have made for a happy working environment."

"They must have been so dedicated to the work that they let it wash over them," surmised Ron.

"Not all of them," commented Henry wryly.

"Why? Who else was there who felt the rough edge of Malcolm's tongue?"

"Have you met Anne?" asked Henry.

"Anne?" queried Tania. "No, we haven't met her yet. We've heard her spoken of by Leah. Anne ...?"

"Anne Langford."

"Of course. The 'mother hen', Leah called her. We've seen her from afar up at the dig."

"Yes, and if you remember, love, Professor Wilton seemed rather dismissive of her at the time," pointed out Ron.

"Huh!" snorted Henry. "Dismissive wasn't the half of it when it came to Sutherland. Because I was down in the farmyard putting away some halters I'd just finished cleaning, and I was just close by the door of the hay-barn when Anne appeared in the doorway. And I heard Sutherland's voice coming from inside, and he was shouting at her, and he said 'If you're going to show me finds, at least make sure you've cleaned them up properly. Maybe at your age you should be getting some new glasses. Now get back up to the dig, and if you can't manage the hill at a decent speed, perhaps you should invest in a walker at the same time.' And Anne rushed past me and disappeared through the gate, but I could see that she was crying as she went."

"How could he speak to someone like that?" said Ron, aghast. "If that'd been me, I'd have smacked him in the face."

"She's too nice," said Henry. "Everybody else

loves her. She's always doing little things for other people, like producing cakes. And she's always the first one to the kettle to make a brew."

"And by my reckoning, that just leaves the younger members of the team," observed Tania. "Anything to report there?"

"I feel sorry for the lad," remarked Henry. "Bless the boy, he's doing his best, and he can't hide the fact that he's helplessly smitten with young Victoria. Not that you'd blame him. She's a very pretty girl. And very bright."

"And him?"

"Oh, there's nothing wrong with him. There's no way he's stupid, or he wouldn't be at Camford, would he?" asked Henry reasonably. "I've no idea about his work, but that wasn't why he was on the receiving end of Sutherland's sniping."

"So why, then?" asked Tania.

"The fact is, he's shy. I've seen them when the whole crew's gone down to the Drover's after finishing up a couple of times ..."

"Didn't Leah tell us that you're living there?" said Ron. "With your young lady, I think she said. The one who does the cleaning of the holiday lets for Leah."

"That's right," replied Henry, slightly gruff. "We rub along together just fine, Jane and I. She works behind the bar there, and I help out some evenings if they're busy. And I've seen young Stephen with Victoria, and he always seems to end up tongue-tied and red in the face. And I'm not the only one to have seen it, because one night I was clearing some glasses from the tables, and that Sutherland chap was having words with Stephen. I didn't hear much in passing, but the gist of it was that the boy shouldn't bother trying to get any closer to Victoria, and maybe he'd have better luck with the alpacas instead of girls."

Tania shook her head in disbelief. "I cannot

fathom how someone that Leah described as so charming on the surface could have such a mean personality underneath."

"That's some pretty unpleasant character flaw," concurred Ron. "It seems almost as if the man was setting himself up as a target."

"But why would he do that?" wondered Tania. "And I'm sure he would never have anticipated how things turned out. The arrogance of power, I suppose."

"And on that note," said Ron, "can I suggest we abandon the unedifying subject of Malcolm Sutherland's character and concentrate on what we're supposed to be doing, which is enjoying a pleasant stroll with these charming animals? What do you say, Santiago?" he added, giving his alpaca a tentative pat on the nose.

"You're absolutely right," smiled Tania. "It's a beautiful day, and the scenery is gorgeous, and I'm sure Henry would rather be telling us about the points of interest along the way."

"Happy to do that, ma'am," said Henry with an answering smile. "In fact, just down there, by the pool ..."

He was interrupted by a hoarse whisper from Ron, his attention caught by a sudden brilliant flash of blue. "Look, love! Quick! Perched on that branch."

"And that," said Henry in hushed tones, "is our resident kingfisher. You're lucky - not everybody gets to see him. And if you wait a second ... there he goes."

The bird dived into the pool, emerging moments later with a wriggling fish in its beak, only to vanish as swiftly as it came.

"Oh, that was wonderful," marvelled Tania. "Henry, have you got any more treats in store for us?"

"Maybe," replied Henry. "There's a family of red squirrels living just down the valley. Not many of those left in these parts. But you'll need to be very quiet."

"We can manage that," answered Ron. "And our animal friends here don't seem to make a lot of noise, so let's go. Henry, you're the boss."

The little group carried on, and were soon lost to sight amidst the dappled shade of the trees.

Chapter 11

"I am," said Ron, almost falling on to the sofa, "if you will pardon the expression, cream-crackered. How many miles have we walked?"

"Oh, dozens, probably," smiled Tania airily. "But you have to admit, it was wonderful."

"That I grant you," replied Ron. "And against you, Henry, and the alpacas, I feel almost ashamed at my lack of stamina."

"But the wildlife," enthused Tania. "That kingfisher. And the flock of bustards that suddenly emerged out of the long grass. And I couldn't believe we actually saw those baby squirrels running around."

"Kits, love," Ron corrected her with a grin. "And Henry did say, or rather whisper, that they're an incredibly rare sight, so we were lucky. Maybe it was the calming aura emitted by the alpacas."

"They were very well-behaved, weren't they? I wouldn't mind going for another walk with them if we get the chance."

"Can we wait until I've recovered from this particular outing?" protested a smiling Ron. "When my dogs have finished barking, as my old grandad used to say. But we made it round, even though my feet are killing me." The smile faded. "And now I've reminded myself about what we're really here for. Finding out, if we can, about the killing of Malcolm Sutherland. What happened? Although we know the 'what'. It's the 'why'."

"And we have more information on that front," Tania reminded him. "Look, why don't you take your shoes off, I'll make us a cup of tea, and then we can go through what we discovered from Henry."

"Good idea, love," said Ron. "Now, are you sure you can find the kettle?"

"Cheek!" riposted Tania. "For that you get no biscuits." She disappeared into the kitchen.

Minutes later, having placed a tray of tea-things on the low table in front of them, Tania joined her husband on the sofa and snuggled up to him. "How are the aching feet?" she enquired.

"Throbbing slightly less," replied Ron. "It's my aching brain that I'm worried about. I'm probably in danger of information overload."

"Let's just recap on what Henry told us bit by bit," suggested Tania, "although I'm getting a pattern, which means that there will be quite a lot of the same as we've heard already."

Ron took a drink of tea. "Right. I am fortified. Over to you, Miss Marple."

"What puzzles me," mused Tania, "is what exactly Malcolm hoped to gain by being so ruthlessly unpleasant to everyone. I mean, take George Cheverell, for instance. Now when we met him, we were quite taken by his enthusiasm for his subject. There's a man who loves history. And he apparently couldn't wait to volunteer when he found out about the dig. And you'd think, with that little museum of his, that he's not completely clueless about what's what. But yet Malcolm Sutherland, it seems, had no respect for his knowledge at all, and what Henry overheard confirms that. More or less a repeat of what Billy Charlton told us in the pub."

"Sounds like a classic case of looking a gift horse in the mouth," remarked Ron.

"More like sending it off to the knacker's yard," said Tania. "He didn't value George at all."

"There's somebody else he didn't value, and that's Edward Wilton," pointed out Ron. "I don't know if he felt at all threatened by him with regard to his leadership of the expedition ..."

"With the sort of arrogance that Malcolm was displaying, I very much doubt it," said Tania.

"And surely Malcolm couldn't have been jealous of Edward for having been given the Professorship of

Archaeology at Camford. Very much the reverse, I would have thought. Nobody has said that Malcolm was in the running for it. Anyway, the way Henry tells it, Edward didn't rise to the bait when Malcolm was sounding off about his unfitness for the job."

"Does that mean he was simply biding his time?" reflected Tania. "Revenge being a dish best served cold, and all that?"

"There was one person who wasn't unaffected by Malcolm's unpleasantness," said Ron, "and that was Anne Langford."

"We must get around to meeting her," said Tania. "We really don't know a thing about her or her personality."

"Other than the fact, from what we've heard, that she seems to be generally liked," observed Ron.

"But not by Malcolm Sutherland. Again, no respect for the woman, and perfectly prepared to demean her efforts without any thought of the consequences."

"Well, Henry saw the consequences," said Ron. "She went off in floods of tears after one of Malcolm's characteristic rants. Not, by the way, that he was alone in thinking less of her than she deserves. We've heard Edward Wilton speaking to her in less than gracious terms."

"Except that Edward has not been discovered lying face down in the dirt, so whatever issues Anne may have with him, they may not be relevant to our thinking at this point."

"Unless he turns up dead," smiled Ron grimly. "That would give us a pattern of behaviour."

"Which I am pushing firmly to one side," replied Tania. "Sufficient unto the day. When we speak to her, we'll be able to gauge that particular potential danger."

"Okay," shrugged Ron. "So, one more snippet from Henry to consider, and that's what he overheard between Malcolm and Stephen Tisbury."

"Not much to go on there. Just a passing remark."

"Yes, but there were overtones - personal ones," pointed out Ron. "Put that together with what we might deduce from what Billy told us about the encounter in the pub corridor, plus Leah's description of Malcolm going after, and I quote, 'anything with a pulse', and was it the sniping comment from somebody who'd had their advances rebuffed and didn't much like it?"

"Yes, but that would give Malcolm a possible reason for wishing Stephen ill, and not the other way around," observed Tania. "Which doesn't make a lot of sense. And we've heard more than once that Stephen is inclined to be shy, plus he's apparently head-over-heels taken with Victoria. Could it possibly be that he had some idea that Malcolm regarded Victoria as one of his targets, being possessed with a pulse, so Stephen became filled with a jealous rage and did Malcolm in? Worms having been known to turn."

"I think we may be straying a bit too far into the realms of speculation, love," smiled Ron. "For a start, we have no evidence that Malcolm had his beady, not to mention sleazy, eye on Victoria - rather the reverse, by what Billy told us - and we haven't any direct evidence as to what Stephen is really like, not having spoken to him."

"Which we should remedy," said Tania. "And no time like the present. So let's finish our tea, you can put your shoes back on," - a faint groan from Ron - "and we'll see if we can track him down."

"May I propose an alternative plan?" suggested Ron. "My dogs are no longer barking quite so loudly, but my stomach has started growling. After all, you can't expect a man to walk halfway across southern England without sustenance, and breakfast seems an awfully long time ago. So how about if I rustle us up some sandwiches - I noticed some rather attractive-looking mature Cheddar in the fridge, and an artisan bloomer alongside it, and there's pickle - and then I'd love to put my head down for half-an-hour's siesta. Alone!" he added hastily, in response to Tania's suspicious raised eyebrow. "After which we shall both be refreshed and revived, firing on all cylinders, and we can go on a Stephen hunt. Deal?" He regarded his wife with eyes that would not have been out of place on an appealing puppy.

"Mr Faye, you are shameless," conceded Tania with a laugh. "I will confess that a cheese sandwich does sound like a good idea. I hadn't realised that I was hungry. So then you may have your siesta, poor decrepit old gentleman that you are, and we'll get back on the mission."

"Snack lunch coming up!" declared Ron, jumping to his feet. "Ow!"

*

It seemed only minutes later that Ron opened his eyes in the dim light of the curtained bedroom to find Tania at his side shaking him gently.

"Oh, that's never been half-an-hour," he yawned.

"You're absolutely right," smiled his wife. "More like three, actually. I looked in on you and you were sleeping like a baby - in fact, I'm not too sure that you weren't sucking your thumb - so I decided to let you sleep. You must have needed it. But the afternoon is wasting away, and we have things to do."

"Okay," said Ron, pushing himself upright. "Give me two seconds to stick my head under a cold tap, and I'm yours."

A few minutes later the couple were standing at the front door of The Byre, just in time to see Stephen Tisbury coming through the gate in the corner of the farmyard which gave on to the path leading up to the dig.

"Leave this to me," hissed Tania to Ron. "Hello there!" she hailed the young man. "Stephen, isn't it? Good afternoon." She took a look at her watch. "Or should that be evening? We were just contemplating popping up to the dig to see if there were any fresh revelations since yesterday."

Stephen gave a tentative smile. "Actually, I suppose it's more like evening. And Professor Wilton has called a halt to work for today, so there's nobody up there now. The others have all come back down already, but he left me to close everything up and put things away, ready for tomorrow."

"Oh, what a shame." Tania exuded disappointment. "Tell me, have you made any progress?"

"A bit," replied Stephen. "Things may be starting to emerge in the main chamber, so the professor thought we should go at it afresh tomorrow."

"How exciting," said Tania. She made as if a thought had suddenly occurred to her. "I'll tell you what. We were just thinking about having a cup of tea. Why don't you join us, and then you can tell us the latest news."

"But it looked as if you were just going out."

"No, no," denied Tania stoutly. "Just coming back. Oh, do come in and bring us up to date."

"I'm a bit grubby."

"Oh, we shan't worry about a bit of dirt on the carpet," said Ron.

"Well, if you're sure it's no trouble ..." hesitated Stephen.

"Not at all," Ron assured him. "I may even be able to find some biscuits as a reward for all your hard work." He led the way into the cottage and made for the kitchen, while Tania ushered the slightly reluctant young archaeologist inside and seated him on the sofa.

"So," said Tania, above the clatter of preparations emanating from the kitchen, "the main chamber, you say?"

"Yes," said Stephen. "We've cleared the entrance, and it looks as if the main structure hasn't collapsed, which was always a worry. Professor Wilton says we're going to need extra lights, so he's getting in touch with the university to have some sent up in the morning. We're hoping that we're about to discover the burial of a tribal chieftain."

"A tribal chieftain, eh?" echoed Ron, arriving with a tray of tea things. "That sounds fascinating."

"It is," nodded Stephen. His brow clouded. "There's just one worrying thing. There was some loose soil and rubble when we cleared the entrance, and the professor is afraid that the tomb may have been disturbed at some point. We can't tell when, at the moment. It could have been ages ago."

"Treasure hunters, I suppose?" guessed Ron. A nod in reply. "You'll have to hope for the best," he said, handing round cups of tea. "Help yourself to sugar if you want it. So, this tribal chieftain. Any idea of who it might have been?"

"Professor Wilton says it's too early to say," said Stephen.

"And what about Professor Sutherland?" enquired Ron. "What were his thoughts on the subject?"

Stephen suddenly became very still. "I ... I really couldn't say."

"Ron!" protested Tania. "That's not a very tasteful question, considering the circumstances. After all, Professor Sutherland has only been dead a couple of days, and I'm sure that everyone must still be feeling very raw at the fact that he was murdered."

"Sorry, love." Ron's apparent contrition was perfectly gauged. "Didn't think."

"You must all have been very shocked," suggested Tania. "In a close team like yours, I mean. And I suppose you have no idea what happened?"

"No, none at all," declared Stephen. "We were all together when we went up to the dig and found him, and that's what we told the police when they came back asking us questions."

"The police have been back here? When?" asked Tania, surprised.

"This morning. That Inspector Copper and his sergeant."

"We had no idea," said Ron. "We were out with Henry on an alpaca walk. A very long alpaca walk," he added under his breath. "So what did they want?"

"They wanted to know when each of us had last seen Professor Sutherland."

"And that's one thing we haven't asked people," murmured Ron in an aside to his wife. "So what happened?" he continued aloud.

"They had each of us in on our own in the finds barn," explained Stephen. "I just told them that I'd seen the professor earlier on Saturday, but I couldn't tell them much." A shadow of a smile crossed his face. "It was quite funny really. The sergeant was supposed to be making notes, but he kept looking sideways at the skeletons where they were laid out. I think he was a bit spooked by them. But I've no idea what anyone else said."

"I dare say the police were trying to build a picture of the dead man and his last movements. Tell me, what sort of man was Professor Sutherland?" enquired Tania. "Did he seem to you the sort of man who might have had enemies?"

"I ... I don't know," responded Stephen. "I didn't actually have all that much to do with him."

"No?" said Tania. "Only I got the impression that you might have chatted to him outside the confines of the dig, so I wondered if you might have got to know him a little."

"I don't know what you mean." Stephen reddened.

"Didn't someone at the pub say they saw you in conversation with him on a couple of occasions? I'd have thought a social environment like that would be the perfect opportunity to break the ice and get closer to somebody."

"They must have got it wrong," replied Stephen. He was plainly reluctant to say more.

"So everything strictly on a professional basis, then? Oh well - it just goes to show you can never rely on things people tell you second-hand," smiled Tania. "So I suppose you'd have no idea as to how well Professor Sutherland got on with the other members of your expedition? Professor Wilton, for instance? Who must be delighted now that he's in charge, although of course he'd wish that the circumstances were less tragic. Did he and Professor Sutherland work well together?"

"I really didn't pay attention," asserted Stephen. "They were in charge. I just got on with whatever job I was told to do."

"As did the other members of the team, I imagine," said Tania. "One big happy family, so to speak. So no harsh words between the professor and any of your colleagues?"

"You couldn't actually say that," admitted Stephen. Tania regarded him enquiringly, and he continued, "I mean, he had pretty high standards. If something wasn't done properly, he let you know. But that would be the same with any team leader on an important job, I suppose. But this is my first dig, so I wouldn't know."

"But nothing personal, then?"

"Oh!" A sudden thought seemed to have struck Stephen.

"You've remembered something?" coaxed Ron.

Stephen shrugged. "It might have been nothing, I suppose. In fact, when I think of it, I don't think it can have been anything serious."

"But you never know. Tell us," urged Tania.

"It was just something I overheard up at the dig. I'd been put on checking through the spoil heap to make sure nothing small had been missed - that tends to be my job - and Professor Sutherland and Mary, Leah's manager, were coming out of the barrow, because apparently Leah had sent her up to see how things were getting on, and it was obviously halfway through a conversation, because she said something like 'Over my dead body', and he replied 'Or mine, I suppose'. But the thing is, it must have been some sort of a joke, because he laughed. Quite loudly, actually. Everybody looked. And when I think of it, that's the only time I ever heard him laugh."

"Difficult to know what to make of that," said Tania. "Not knowing the context, I mean. Although it is a little eerie to think that he was found dead shortly afterwards. And you can't think of anything similar with regard to the rest of the farm staff? Or any of your colleagues?"

Stephen shook his head. "No."

"So you'd have no idea whether any of them had any sort of problem with Professor Sutherland?" pressed Tania. "No personality clashes? Nobody in particular who didn't meet his standards? Because you did say that he was pretty demanding. And not everybody can cope with that, can they?" A significant pause. "However intimate the nature of those demands may be."

Stephen got suddenly to his feet. "Look, I really have to go. I need to take a shower. Thank you for the tea." He plonked his cup back on the tray with a crash. "I ... goodbye." He blundered his way out of the cottage, leaving Tania and Ron looking at one another, surprised at the speed of his departure.

Chapter 12

"And what, I wonder, does all that tell us?" mused Tania eventually.

"You tell me," returned Ron. "That was a right old mixture of lies and evasions, in my opinion."

"Ah," said Tania, "but why do people lie and evade? That's the question."

"Because they have something to hide."

"But what are they hiding? Is it guilt because they've done something they don't want the world to find out about? Murder springs to mind. Do we have enough potential motives to say that Stephen Tisbury is in the frame?"

"Possibly," said Ron. "And the number one of those could well be that conversation in the pub, where Malcolm Sutherland threatened Stephen because he seems to have been reluctant to ... well, let's not go into details."

"And reluctant because it's plain that, from what we've heard, Stephen was hopelessly taken with Victoria. He didn't lie about what he did, but about what he didn't do. And we also know, from what we've heard, that Malcolm's attitude towards Victoria was far from kindly. Could Stephen have witnessed something between Malcolm and Victoria," wondered Tania, "where he saw that she was threatened in some regard, so he felt protective towards her and acted accordingly?"

"That's speculation, but it's quite a reasonable one," agreed Ron. "We know that, by the sound of it, Victoria's academic future was in jeopardy." Ron slapped his forehead. "And that's what that remark of his in the pub about 'No Masters in her future' meant. Billy didn't click, but I just have. Malcolm could have used his influence to scupper Victoria's hopes of gaining higher qualifications. And as we know from previous cases, the urge to protect a loved one is just as powerful a motive for murder as the wish to protect oneself."

"Good thought," said Tania. "And then there's Stephen's refusal to admit to any of the other indications of the general nastiness of Malcolm to his team. All right, maybe he wouldn't want to confess to being on the receiving end of bullying himself, because he'd be afraid that it might make him look weak. But he came close to defending Malcolm's style, on account of the man's allegedly high work standards. That rings hopelessly untrue, and it's not as if he's in any danger of backlash from Malcolm if he chose to speak out." Tania frowned.

"Actually, he did speak out, and that was when he told us about that incident between Malcolm and Mary," pointed out Ron. "So was he attempting to point the finger away from himself, even though he passed it off as a joke? Was it a sudden case of improvisation to deflect questions?"

"You and I both know that improvisation is one of the more difficult theatrical skills," remarked Tania drily. "No, I think I'm tempted to take him at his word. For that incident at least."

"So we're no further forward," sighed Ron.

"Maybe we've got one or two more jigsaw pieces," replied Tania. "But nowhere near the complete puzzle, and that's because we still haven't finished our harmless chats with everyone."

"I'd be interested to hear Inspector Copper's comments on your definition of a 'harmless chat'," laughed Ron. "So, who's your next target for this ruthless interrogation?"

"Plainly, Anne Langford," said Tania. "She's the one remaining team member that we haven't spoken to, and we know next to nothing about her."

"Other than that she's everyone's favourite mother-figure. Except, of course, Malcolm Sutherland's."

"So let's go and find out why," suggested Tania, getting briskly to her feet.

"Just a thought," said Ron, as the couple emerged from the front door of The Byre. "Where are we likely to find Anne Langford? If Edward Wilton's called a halt to work for the day, she's not going to be up at the barrow, is she?."

"And since we don't know which cottage she's staying in, we'd better go and ask Leah," said Tania. "In any case, it might be a good idea to have a word with her anyway. If the police have been back up here interviewing everybody, as Stephen said, then she must have been on their list. Who knows, they may have given her an idea as to how their enquiries are going."

"I think I know," replied Ron. "Because remembering how tight-lipped your Inspector Copper has been in the past, he's not going to be giving out information willy-nilly, is he?"

Tania shrugged. "We can but hope." She crossed the farmyard to the door of the farmhouse and knocked.

"Oh, you again," was Leah's less than welcoming reaction when she answered the door. "Sorry, that doesn't sound very nice, but I had a horrible feeling it was the police come back to pester me."

"Only us," smiled Ron. "I confess we're after some information, but we're not planning an interrogation."

"You'd better come in," said Leah, and ushered her guests into the sitting room. "So, what was it you were wanting?"

"We heard that the inspector had come back asking questions this morning," said Tania. "Which we knew nothing about, having been off walking with Henry and the alpacas."

"How did that go?" enquired Leah. "Which beasts did you take? And did you enjoy it?"

"Far more than we imagined we would," replied Tania. "I had Lima, and Ron had Santiago, and we must have gone for miles. And we saw lots of wildlife. We had a really good time." She cast a sympathetic look in her husband's direction. "Apart from Ron's feet, which were complaining by the time we got back. But all in all it was very instructive."

"So now you're up on all the flora and fauna of Wessex?" said Leah.

"Not so much that. It was more a case of hearing what Henry had to say about what's gone on around here in the run-up to Malcolm's death. Because he witnessed a few things which could be pointers as to why Malcolm met his end."

"That's the thing about the staff," observed Leah. "Very often the visitors are so full of the excitement of the experience that they forget the staff are there. I've heard tales of couples having full-blown rows with Jane or Mary standing not two feet away."

"Well, it was a little like that with Henry," remarked Ron. "He overheard quite a few exchanges between Malcolm and the dig team. Mind you, most of what he told us simply reinforced the picture we already had of him, but every little helps to form the picture."

"You mean the picture of an ill-mannered male chauvinist bully?" said Leah, with an unexpected grin. "Oh, all right, I know I should have told you more about him at the start, but I didn't want to influence your thinking. And I'll admit it took me a little while to figure out the sort of man he was when we were together. But even with all his faults, we did manage to have a few good times - if I dig deep enough in my memory banks, that is - and he didn't deserve to end up the way he did."

"How much of that did you share with Inspector Copper when he came calling?" wondered Tania.

"Actually, he was remarkably uninterested in our personal history, once he'd accepted that there was no way I could have been involved in Malcolm's murder," said Leah. "What he was mostly after was details of when I'd last seen Malcolm on the day of his death, and once I'd convinced him that I was well off the scene, he went away to quiz everybody else."

"So we gather," said Tania. "We've been speaking to Stephen Tisbury, and he gave us the same story. In fact, he reminded us that that's one question we haven't been asking people, so we may have to retrace our steps and slide that into the conversation somehow. But at the moment, we're still trying to complete our list of people, because we haven't yet spoken to Anne Langford."

"And the thing is, we don't know where she's staying," added Ron. "Stephen told us they've packed up for the day, so we're going to have to go and knock on her door. Except that we don't know which door to knock at."

"Oh, that's easy," replied Leah. "She's staying in Tumulus Cottage, sharing with Victoria. It's the one just on the corner of the yard with the green front door. Turn right out of here, and you can't miss it."

"Then that's exactly what we'll do," said Tania, getting to her feet.

"I think I can make it that far," said Ron, joining her. "And I also reckon I can probably manage to totter as far as the pub this evening. I am well overdue for a pint."

*

The door was opened by a comfortably-built mature woman who regarded her visitors with an enquiring smile.

"Anne Langford?" said Tania.

"That's right." The smile was enhanced by a twinkle in the eye. "And I know who you are. You're Leah's friends, aren't you? The ones who are going around asking questions."

"Guilty as charged," admitted Ron. "Can you spare us a few minutes?"

"You'd better come in," said Anne. "Go through into the sitting room." She indicated a sofa. "And do sit down. I was wondering when you were going to get around to me."

"You were?" asked Tania, slightly taken aback by the tone of the welcome.

"We don't live in hermetically sealed compartments up at the dig, you know," replied Anne. "We do speak to one another - that's when we haven't got the management breathing down our necks to get on with whatever the next task may be. So I realised that the innocent chats that Leah's friends were having with my colleagues had some purpose, and that was obviously to find the identity of Malcolm Sutherland's murderer. Leah evidently didn't feel that the police effort was sufficient. And am I not right in thinking that you come from Ramston?"

"We do," said Ron.

"I may be hopelessly mistaken, and barking up the completely wrong tree, but wasn't there something in the paper a while ago concerning one of the academics from Camford? A murder at Ramston Abbey that was in part solved by a local librarian. It was the Camford reference that caught my eye. I don't suppose, by some remote chance, that you work in the library at Ramston, do you, Tania?"

Tania gave a rueful grin. "It seems I've been busted before we even start," she said. "Perhaps, Mrs Langford, you ought to be doing my job."

"As amateur sleuth, you mean," smiled Anne. "Not what I'm cut out for. I prefer my dead bodies to have some age to them. And by the way, it's Anne."

"And this is not going the way I expected it to, Anne," said Tania.

"Life is full of surprises," responded Anne. "Now, before we get down to things, can I offer you a cup of tea?"

"You're very kind," said Ron, "but if I have any more tea today I shall probably go off pop."

"Perhaps something with a little more character?" twinkled Anne. "I did take the precaution of bringing a rather nice bottle of scotch with me from home. I do like a bedtime snifter."

Ron smiled at Tania. "Now here is a woman after my own heart, love."

"I'll get the glasses." Anne busied herself producing bottle and glasses from a cupboard, poured three generous measures, and then seated herself once more and directed her gaze towards Tania. "So, what would you like to know?"

"Well, you spoke of dead bodies, so we obviously have to talk about the most recent one. Tell me, how did things stand between you and Malcolm Sutherland?"

"Ghastly man," responded Anne without hesitation. "He really was one of the most unpleasant individuals it's ever been my misfortune to work in conjunction with."

"Now let's not have any pussy-footing around," chuckled Ron. "Why don't you say what you really mean."

"I am not a believer in never speaking ill of the dead," stated Anne crisply. "You never get to the truth that way. And from what I saw of Malcolm Sutherland, he was always one to speak ill of the living if he got the opportunity."

"Any examples spring to mind?" enquired Tania.

"Probably too many to list," said Anne. "I lost count of the number of times I heard him speak rudely to one or other of my colleagues. Casting doubt on their professional abilities or personal qualities - it was all grist to his mill."

"Do you each have a particular job on the dig?" wondered Ron.

"Loosely. Professor Wilton does most of the initial digging, and George joins in whenever he can grab the chance. He even used to bring his own trowel," she added with a chuckle. "Terrible old thing. Victoria concentrates on the finds, because bones are her thing, and Stephen tends to get the donkey work like sifting the spoil heap.

As for me, I'm just the old scrubber."

"Sorry?" frowned Ron, perplexed.

Anne laughed. "That just means I'm sat there a lot of the time in the tent with a toothbrush and a bowl of water, scrubbing the dirt off any finds. While wearing those attractive white rubber gloves. Marigolds they aren't."

"Thank goodness for that."

"And Professor Sutherland spent most of his time swanning around being supervisory and passing remarks on people's efforts."

"Including yourself?"

"Oh, I didn't escape. I was on the receiving end of my fair share. Fortunately, I have broad shoulders."

"Actually," said Ron, "we did an alpaca walk with Henry this morning ..."

"I like Henry," broke in Anne. "He's something of an old-fashioned gentleman. Always tips his cap to me with a 'Morning, ma'am' whenever our paths cross. Hasn't always a great deal to say for himself, but he's always pleasant. And he loves those animals."

"That's the impression we got this morning," said Tania. "And fortunately he wasn't too taciturn during our walk. He did reveal a few incidents he'd witnessed - including one which apparently left you in tears. So maybe shoulders not all that broad ...?" Tania paused expectantly.

"Do you know, you're absolutely right," said Anne. "To tell the truth, I had probably put it to the back of my mind. It doesn't do to dwell on such things, does it? There's always the danger they may fester. But yes, there was an occasion when there had been a find in the spoil heap - I can't even remember exactly what it was - and Stephen drew it to my attention, and it looked to me as if it might be quite interesting, so I trotted back down here, because I knew Professor Sutherland was working in the finds barn, but when I showed it to him, he was distinctly unimpressed. And gratuitously insulting too. I may be the oldest member of the team, but I've still got all my marbles." A wintery smile. "All my own teeth too. So it came as something of a shock that he would be quite so brutal to my face."

"I imagine it would," sympathised Tania. "Henry did give us the gist of what passed between you."

"But heigh ho, I've probably had worse said to me in my time," said Anne with determined cheerfulness. "And even Professor Wilton can be a little sharp at times. But I've learnt to shrug things off. Sadly, I don't know that the same can be said for the younger members of the team. They do speak to me, and I have the distinct impression that they've been on the receiving end of what I can only call Professor Sutherland's bile."

"You don't think there may have been an element of thwarted attraction in Sutherland's attitude?" hazarded Tania.

"With Victoria?" responded Anne. "I hadn't thought of that. I suppose it's possible She's a pretty girl." Tania waited with eyebrows raised and a meaningful look. "What, you mean with Stephen too? Good lord! Now that's a thought that never crossed my mind." She reflected for a moment. "So you believe that either one of them might have reacted to unwelcome advances in a violent way?"

Tania shrugged. "I don't think anything is too far-fetched to consider. But as we've heard from other people, the youngsters weren't the only ones with reasons to feel ill-will towards the professor. Although nobody has been as frank as you."

"So am I hiding my own murderous thoughts behind a facade of truthfulness?" asked Anne with a dry smile. "I suppose you could make out a convincing case against me if you put your mind to it."

"I haven't had the chance as yet to make out a convincing case against anyone," returned Tania. "I just want to help Leah, so I'm still asking questions. As I believe the police did earlier today when they came calling."

"They did," said Anne. "They didn't quite have us all lined up against a wall, but they did call each of us in individually to quiz us. Making sure our stories tallied, I suppose."

"And asking when you last saw Professor Sutherland, I believe."

"They did. And, in fact, it was probably the easiest topic on which we could all agree, because it was on the return trip from the pub on Saturday night."

"You were all down at the Drover's together?" enquired Ron. "I'm starting to wonder how jolly these social get-togethers would have been, given that Professor Sutherland had not been exactly charming to each of you at various times."

"Oh, he could switch on the charm when it suited him," replied Anne. "Fake charm, of course. I could see through it."

"So what was the occasion?" wondered Tania. "Or just the end of the working week?"

"No, actually. It was because the moment had come when we were about to break into the main chamber of the barrow. Something of a landmark. And in fact, Professor Sutherland had made a start, but then he suddenly announced that we'd leave it for now. George Cheverell wanted to carry on - he was very keen - but the professor hauled him away and said we should begin anew the next morning. Practically insisted that we all leave the site immediately and, once we'd had a chance to freshen up, go to the pub together. So that's what we did. He even bought a round of drinks. Unheard of!"

"So coming back to the last time you saw the professor ..." coaxed Tania.

"We all left the pub together and headed back up the hill. In fact, I'm sure we were the last to leave, with

Jane and Henry virtually pushing us out of the door so that they could lock up. I think they were having a late supper with the landlord. Of course, George peeled off *en route* because his cottage is on the way, but then we all came back to the farm and more or less all disappeared into our various accommodations simultaneously. And I for one didn't see or hear anything until the next day when we all gathered together to go back up to the barrow, at which point somebody realised that Professor Sutherland was not among us. And I dare say you know what happened next."

Chapter 13

"Do you find," asked Ron, as he and Tania strolled down the lane in the direction of Upson Parva, "that detecting gives you an appetite and a thirst?"

"You don't need an excuse to want to go to the pub, darling," laughed Tania. "It's a perfectly normal human activity. Especially since it's been quite a few hours since we had anything for lunch."

"Although I'm not sure I'm up for another helping of rook pie," responded Ron with a grin. "Once is probably enough. I'm more in the mood for something more conventional, like sausage and chips washed down with a pint of Ferret's Firkin, or whatever else Billy Charlton has on tap."

"I'm sure they'll be able to oblige."

Ron's brow clouded. "Just one potential fly in the ointment. It would be a tad inconvenient if we run into the entire dig team out for their habitual evening session at the boozer."

"I suspect," replied Tania, "that that particular habit may well have fallen by the wayside, in the light of recent events. Can't you imagine everyone sitting around in an uneasy circle looking askance at one another and not wanting to be the first to break the silence."

"Hmmm. Awkward," nodded Ron. "Let's hope you're right. Because if we come face-to-face with them *en masse*, our cover as innocent tourists is definitely going to be blown. We shall have to hope for the best." He held the pub door open for his wife, and the two of them made their way into the bar of the Drover's Rest.

"Evening, darlings," came the greeting from the woman behind the bar. Looking to be in her forties, buxom and attractive, with her bright blonde hair in an immaculately-sculpted 1940s style and wearing a tightly-cinched skirt and a frill-necked blouse which stopped just short of being revealing, she gave the newcomers a broad welcoming smile. "And what can I get for you?"

Ron hoisted himself on to a bar stool and gave his wife a brief consulting glance. "A G and T for the lady, and I'll have a pint of ... what can you suggest? And I've already sampled a pint of your Drover's Draught, which is a fine brew but I'm not sure I could manage two, so what else is on offer?"

"How about Wessex Wonder? That's a bit lighter."

"Sounds good."

"Coming up, darling." The barmaid turned away. "So, not from round here, then?" she enquired over her shoulder. "Staying local, are you?"

"Yes," replied Tania. "We're in one of the cottages in the farm up the hill."

"Oh, *that's* who you are," said the barmaid, depositing the drinks in front of the couple. "In which case, I know who you are. You're Mr and Mrs Faye, aren't you?"

"And if I'm not much mistaken," said Tania with an answering smile, "you must be Jane."

"That's right," nodded the barmaid. "Jane Sherrington."

"Because Leah mentioned you," continued Tania. "We're old friends of hers. And she told us that you work here at the pub when you're not doing some cleaning work for her at the cottages."

"And for a few other people round the village," confirmed Jane. "But I have to say, of all the places I've cleaned over the years, yours is the neatest I've ever come across. It only takes me five minutes to do your cottage. Not like some of the others up there now. Honestly, some people are so untidy. Especially that young boy ... what's his name?"

"Stephen?"

"That's the one. All his clothes all over the floor anyhow. And the bathroom – well, don't ask. I'd like to have a good long talk with his mother about the way she brought him up, I can tell you."

"I'm pleased I meet your high standards," smiled Ron. "Years of doing the housework under the beady eye of my dear wife."

"Ignore him, Jane," laughed Tania. "We both hate a mess."

"Well, you've arrived in the middle of a right mess up at the farm," said Jane in subdued tones. "Of course, you know what's gone on up there?"

Tania lowered her voice to match. "We do. In fact, that's the reason we're here. Leah asked us if we could help finding out what's happened, because we've been involved in one or two incidents before. And in fact, we'd be grateful if you were able to shed any light on the situation."

"Ah, that makes sense," said Jane. "I was chatting to my other half, and he said there were questions being asked, and not just by the police. So that was you two, was it?"

"It was," said Ron. "We met Henry yesterday when he took us for a walk with a couple of the alpacas, and he did let us know a few bits and pieces that could be of interest. I wonder if you might be able to do the same?"

"Course I will," replied Jane readily. "But not now. I've not really got the time to chat when we're busy. But how about when I come up to do your cottage tomorrow morning?"

"That would be perfect," smiled Tania. "Now, as Ron has confessed to feeling peckish, we'd better have a look at your menu."

"Coming right up." Jane darted away, returning in moments with the small slate bearing the evening's choices chalked on it. "Take a look at that, and I'll be back to take your order in two ticks."

*

When Ron answered the sharp rap at the door of

The Byre the following morning, it was to reveal Jane Sherrington, as expected. What was not expected was the complete transformation of their visitor. Gone were the stylish hairstyle and smart top - in their place was a headscarf tied over scraped-back hair, and an all-enveloping overall in pink and yellow checks. Yellow rubber gloves peeped over the rim of a plastic bucket filled with cleaning cloths and sprays.

"Can I do you now, sir?" enquired Jane in a mock Cockney accent.

"Good lord!" laughed Ron. "That's a blast from the past, isn't it? What was it - some wartime radio comedy? Mrs Mop, wasn't it?"

"I love the old comedies," replied Jane. "Much funnier than some of the modern stuff. I like looking them up on the internet. And it's amazing what you can find on *YouSpot*."

"Couldn't agree more," said Ron. "Try taking the mickey out of people these days and you find the thought police banging on your door. But don't get me started on that, or we'll be here all day, and that's not why you're here. Come in, come in." He stood back to admit Jane. "Go on through and sit yourself down."

Jane cast an eye around the sitting room, where Tania was waiting on the sofa. "If I didn't know better, I'd say you've already done my job for me before I arrived," she said, perching on the edge of an armchair.

Tania smiled. "Well, we did have a bit of a tidy-up," she confessed. "And we've made the beds. We decided that if we were going to take up your time picking your brains, the least we could do is not keep you back from your other jobs."

"I wish everyone was so considerate," said Jane. "Some people are. Like that nice lady Mrs Langford in Tumulus. Always has the washing-up done whenever I get there, and she always offers me a cup of tea if she's still in. Old school, you see. That's when people used to have manners. Not like ..." She paused.

Tania leaned forward. "Like Professor Sutherland, were you going to say?" she asked. "Because we've heard a few things from various people."

Jane pulled a face. "The thing is, it goes against the grain to gossip about the guests here. It's not the done thing, and doing my job, you find out quite a few things about people, but I like to think I know when to be discreet. Honestly, the number of times I've walked in on people when they were in the middle of - well, let's just say I could tell some tales."

"That's the thing," said Ron, sitting alongside his wife. "We do actually need you to tell some tales if we're going to help Leah by finding out how Professor Sutherland met his end. Now she knows, and we think the police also know, that it must have been someone who's involved with the dig up on the Downs. There's nobody else who could have had the opportunity. But what is still not clear is what the motive could have been. And we know that there were a number of clashes between the professor and the other people around here, so we're doing our best to see if anything among those could have led to somebody wishing to do him harm."

Jane nodded slowly. "I see that."

"So I'm assuming you've seen or heard something of the kind," said Tania. "For a start, you mentioned Anne Langford. I get the impression that there must have been some incident with the professor that you were witness to?"

"There was," replied Jane. "One night down at the Drover's - don't ask me exactly when. But he was up at the bar getting a drink, and I was chatting to him, because you have to be friendly to the customers, don't you, no matter what you may think of them quietly to yourself. Anyhow, I just asked him how things were going up at the dig, and were they finding anything specially interesting, and he said that things were coming along, although he said it was probably a bit too technical for somebody like me to understand. And I thought 'Get you, Mr High-and-mighty, looking down on us peasants', but I kept smiling, and he said 'Mind you, you wouldn't be the only one. We've got a woman up there that they call a mature student, and she's really not up to it'. And I realised he was talking about Mrs Langford, and at that moment she came up to the bar alongside him. Now he didn't notice her, and I was trying to signal to him with my eyes that she was there, but he didn't take a blind bit of notice, and he carried on, saying 'The old trout's nothing but a passenger', and he'd be glad to be rid of her. And I saw her mouth go tight before she turned away and walked off, and I could see she was upset. And the stupid man never even knew she was there."

"Evidently not a gentleman with a great deal of respect for the ladies," remarked Ron drily.

"You say that," said Jane, now well into her stride, "but it all depends which of the ladies you're talking about."

"Oh?" queried Tania, intrigued. "Who do you mean, I wonder? Or can I guess?"

"If you were to guess our Mary who runs this place for Leah, you wouldn't be wide of the mark," stated Jane.

"I suspected as much," said Tania. "We've heard about Professor Sutherland's advances to her."

"Advances?" snorted Jane. "Well, he might have tried to advance, but she was pretty quick to retreat!"

"Tell us," urged Tania.

"I say 'retreat'," qualified Jane. "It was more like 'repel'. And it happened at the Drover's as well."

"Everything seems to happen at your pub," remarked Ron. "It must be like living in a TV soap, working there."

"Social hub of the village," chuckled Jane. "If it didn't happen there, it probably didn't happen."

"With one or two notable exceptions," pointed out Tania. "Like the Malcolm Sutherland affair."

"Funny you should say that," said Jane, "because an affair is exactly what he had in mind, by the sound of it. See, what happened was, Henry was on his break, so I was going round some tables picking up glasses, and our Mary was sat on her own, because she likes to come in some evenings for a quiet drink. There's a whisky she likes - Glen Whatever-it-is - and we keep a bottle behind the bar specially for her. Anyway, there she was, and all of a sudden that Sutherland bloke is sliding in next to her in her booth, and I was clearing the table in the next booth, so I could hear everything. 'Seems a shame for an attractive young lady to be sitting drinking alone', he was saying, 'and even more so because that looks like a particularly attractive glass of Scotland's finest export'. And she said she preferred to choose her drinking companions, and he said 'What about other companions?', and he said that he had a bottle of very good Scotch in his cottage, and he'd be more than happy to come round to her place that night. 'Perhaps we could share it, and one or two other things besides', he said."

"Not exactly subtle in his approach," observed Ron. "How did Mary react to that? I bet she got hot under the collar."

"Actually, no," replied Jane. "In fact, she gave him the big heave-ho, but very calm. She said he'd set foot in her cottage when hell froze over, and if he ever tried anything, she would not be responsible for her actions. Told him to sling his hook, although she put it rather more ladylike."

"That should have sent him off with his tail between his legs," said Tania.

"Not a bit of it," said Jane. "In fact he laughed, and said he was a patient man and that he could bide his time. And then off he went with a sort of sleazy grin on his face. Horrible man. I'd have given him a good slap if it had been me. And I told Henry about it, but he said not to worry, because Mary was quite capable of looking after herself."

"Any more lively episodes in the life of a country pub?" enquired Ron. "Surely there must be."

"Not that I can think of off-hand," reflected Jane. "But that's not to say that there aren't other bits and pieces I've overheard on and off."

"Which I assume have some sort of bearing on what we're talking about," said Tania. "Because we've come to understand that the dig team was most definitely not one big happy family. The whole thing seems to have been rife with tensions of one kind or another."

"You're not wrong," agreed Jane. "Although it wasn't always face-to-face. I remember one morning, I was in Henge Cottage trying to restore some sort of order to that boy Stephen's bedroom. I know I shouldn't, because it's not as if I'm supposed to pick up after people, but I couldn't bear the state it was in. Anyway, I was upstairs in there, because when I arrived that Professor Wilton was still there doing paperwork or something downstairs. They share the place, the two men. Anyway, Mr Wilton said go on up and make a start upstairs, and he'd be gone shortly, but then I heard the door go, and it was Professor Sutherland. He'd come looking for Mr Wilton because he said that he was sick and tired of the way Victoria was doing her work. 'She's completely useless', he said, 'and I've told her so to her face'. Said she couldn't tell a tibia from a toenail, or some such, and he wanted to know why Mr Wilton was still putting up with her. He said if it was up to him, she'd be gone. And Mr Wilton said that it was just as well that the professor wasn't in charge of the composition of the dig team, and he had the highest regard for Victoria and her work. She'd stay on the team until he decided otherwise. 'Don't you go causing trouble among my people', he said, 'because it could easily come back on you'. Quite a shouting match, it turned into."

"Sounds as if Professor Wilton was very protective of all the Camford team," observed Ron. "He seems to have put his foot down pretty firmly."

"So he may have done," replied Jane, "but I don't think that Professor Sutherland was too impressed. 'Just what I'd expect from someone like you', he said, all sneering-like. And he said goodness knows why the university authorities saw fit to put someone like Mr Wilton in charge of an important department. 'I could do your job so much better than you', he said. And he said 'Do you know what the difference is between you and the skeletons we've unearthed up at the dig? The skeletons have actually got backbones!'. And he must have stormed out, because I heard the front door slam. Fair shook the place, it did."

"It can't have been pleasant, overhearing a confrontation like that," sympathised Tania.

"Not so's you'd notice," responded Jane grimly. "And I wasn't certain what to do. I was sure Mr Wilton had probably forgotten I was still on the premises, so I got on with things as quietly as I could, but then I finished the bathroom, flushed the loo to make sure he knew I was there, and then went back downstairs. And there he was, sat there with his head in his hands. And I just said I was about to make a start on the kitchen, and would he like me to make him a cup of tea while I was at it, and he seemed to come to a bit and said that no, he'd better be getting back up to the dig because there were things he had to do. And then off he went. Didn't seem his normal self, though." She looked at Tania and Ron. "That's about all I can remember about the goings-on between that lot. Honestly, give me normal tourists any time. And alpacas. They never give you aggravation."

"So Henry says," smiled Ron.

"And now I'd better get on giving this place the

once-over," said Jane, getting to her feet.

"Honestly, there's no need," protested Tania. "And we've held you up quite long enough. You must have lots to do in the other cottages, and this place is fine. But thanks a lot for the information. It's going to give us plenty to think about."

Chapter 14

"You weren't wrong," observed Ron, as he closed the front door behind the departing Jane and re-entered the sitting room.

"About what?" enquired Tania absently, her mind evidently elsewhere.

"About having plenty to think about," replied her husband. "But I have a suggestion."

"And what's that?" said Tania, her attention returning to her husband.

"You know the way people come to the farm and go walking with the alpacas because it's said to be a very calming experience."

"Well?" Tania was clearly not following Ron's train of thought.

"I think we ought to do the same. We've been quizzing people virtually non-stop for the last few days, and I for one have a head full of information buzzing around without any clear focus. And I wouldn't mind betting that you're probably the same."

"It's true," agreed Tania with a rueful smile. "All questions, and remarkably few answers as to who might have been responsible for Malcolm Sutherland's murder. Other than everyone, of course. More reasons to dislike the man than we can shake a stick at."

"Precisely," stated Ron. "So my suggestion is, let it all go for a while. Give your brain a rest for a bit. If walking with the alpacas is such a soothing experience, which we know for a fact that it is, let's give it another go. Why don't we go and find Henry and see if he's free to take us on another ramble? Let's face it, he's not exactly going to be run off his feet tending to the needs of visiting tourists, is he? He's more than likely to be glad of the distraction. So what do you say?"

Tania got to her feet and deposited a kiss on her husband's cheek. "I say, my darling," she replied, "that you are a very clever man. I knew there was a reason I married you. So let me exchange these slippers for something sturdier, and we'll seek out Henry right now."

*

"I wish I could," said the alpaca handler, when the couple tracked him down in one of the animal stalls in a small barn. "But I can't get away at the moment because I'm waiting for the vet. Rio here's got a bit of an issue." He indicated a small white alpaca nestling in the straw in one corner.

"Nothing too serious, I hope," said Tania, concern evident in her voice.

"Oh, I think it's just a bit of colic," Henry reassured her. "There's some ivy growing up one of the oak trees, and I suspect that she's been eating that. But I want the vet to take a look at her, just to be on the safe side." He absent-mindedly tousled the animal's curly topknot as she gazed up at him with soulful eyes.

"You concentrate on looking after her," said Ron. "And don't worry about us. We can easily go out with the animals another time."

"Unless ..." said Henry.

"Unless what?"

"Now I wouldn't normally do this, but being as you're friends of Leah's, and seeing how well you got on with the beasts yesterday, I suppose I could let you take Lima and Santiago out by yourselves. You're used to them, and they're used to you. Mind you, you'd need to take the same route as we did together ..."

"Don't worry," said Tania. "I'm sure we can remember the way."

"I don't think it would much matter if you didn't," said Henry with a quiet chuckle. "Those two have been on that walk so many times, they could probably find their way round on their own."

"If you're sure you trust us ...?" said Ron.

Henry seemed to make up his mind. "I do," he

said with a brisk nod. "So let me get hold of a couple of halters, and we'll go up to the field and harness up."

"You do that," said Ron. "In the meantime, I'll nip back indoors. I noticed there's some ham in the fridge, so I'll knock up some sandwiches and grab a bottle of water and a couple of bananas. We can have a picnic on the way round."

"You're brilliant, darling," replied Tania. "Come and find us." She and Henry set out towards the paddocks.

*

"This is a treat," remarked Ron, as the couple made their way out of the farmyard leading the pair of alpacas, who seemed entirely content with the arrangement. In fact, Santiago was happy to take the lead, pulling gently on his leading rein, after a brief but fruitless snuffle around Ron's backpack. "And I'm very sorry to tell you that I'm not carrying any treats for you, mate, so you'll have to manage without. I have an awful suspicion that I'm in charge of our notorious cake bandit of blessed memory," he added in an aside to Tania.

"It looks rather more as if he's in charge of you," she replied with a laugh, as she followed with the considerably more docile Lima. "But the good thing about that is, if we happen to lose our way, I'm sure Santiago will bring us back in one piece. Now, is it here we turn off the road?"

"I think so," said Ron. "This is George Cheverell's cottage, isn't it?"

As if conjured by magic, the owner's head popped up over the garden well with a cheery "Hello, you two!"

"Oh! Good morning, Mr Cheverell," responded Tania in surprise. "Gosh, you made me jump."

"Sorry about that," apologised George, getting to his feet from his kneeling position. "But I always like to say hello to my two woolly friends here whenever they pass. And of course, good morning to you as well, Mr and

Mrs ...?"

"Tania and Ron will do very well," replied Ron. "I'm surprised to see you here. I'd have thought you'd be hard at it up at the dig."

"Yes," said Tania. "We happened to be talking to Stephen Tisbury yesterday, and he mentioned that today was likely to be something of a big day because you were all due to start on the main chamber of the barrow."

"Indeed," nodded George. "But unfortunately, 'all' doesn't include me at the moment. Our great leader decided that, in the absence of the new lights which he thought he had arranged but which didn't turn up this morning, he would make a start on his own, so I and the others were dismissed. I left the rest of them cooling their heels around the site, but I decided I could find better things to do, so I've come back down to tackle the slugs who are making a meal of my bedding plants." He held up a plastic bucket. "My beer traps are doing sterling work so far. So at least there's one good aspect of the situation."

"It sounds as if you're not too happy to be sidelined," observed Tania. "I do hope there aren't any tensions emerging. I'd have thought there had been quite enough of that when Professor Sutherland was in charge. Don't tell me that Professor Wilton is following in his footsteps."

"Oh good lord, no," laughed George with a carefree air. "Nothing of the sort. No, actually I get on very well with Professor Wilton. Just as I did with his predecessor. No, I just hope that he isn't also falling into the trap of wanting to be first on the scene to make some sort of ground-breaking find. Well," he added darkly, "good luck with that."

"Now we mustn't keep you," said Ron, as Santiago seemed disposed to want to look over the garden wall and display an unwelcome interest in George's shrubs. "We'd better get on our way and leave you to your gardening. And I hope you manage to sort out the slugs."

"You have to keep pests under control," responded George obliquely, before disappearing once more behind the garden wall.

"Come along, you," urged Tania to Lima, and she led the alpaca along the path at the side of the cottage in the direction of the woodland behind, with Ron and his companion in her wake.

"It seems to me," remarked Ron, "that we can't seem to leave the topic of Malcolm Sutherland's death alone. Whatever we do, up it pops, so we might as well succumb to the inevitable and chew over things. At least we know that our two friends here won't be laughing at us, however ludicrous some of our ideas may be. So, what do we know?"

"Let's go right back to basics," suggested Tania. "Who can we absolutely rule out as having had anything to do with Malcolm's death?"

"Leah, for a start. Whatever history the two of them may have had together, a) it's pretty much in the dim and distant past, and she swears that there's been no contact between them for yonks, and b) it's provable beyond a shadow of a doubt that she couldn't have been anywhere near the dig site at the crucial time. Not that I believed for a second that she could have been involved. We know her well enough to say that it simply isn't in her nature. But you did say we should go back to basics."

"Happy to do so," smiled Tania. "So then we'll move on to Jane Sherrington and Henry Gifford. Both involved with the farm in one way or another, but it doesn't appear that either of them had much in the way of direct contact with Malcolm, so we'd probably be scratching our heads to find any sort of motive for them. And in addition to that, they were both working at the pub on the fateful evening, and saw the dig party off at closing time, according to Anne Langford. She said those two were due to have a late supper with Billy Charlton and his sons, and in any event they all live at the pub, so unless the two of them, or even all five, are working in cahoots in some sort of conspiracy, I can't see that they shouldn't also be ruled out."

"Seems fair enough." A thought occurred to Ron. "Does that mean we ought to be adding George Cheverell to the list as well? Didn't Anne also mention that he peeled off into his own cottage as the group headed back up the hill? If he's down in Upson Parva, he can't have been wielding a murder weapon up at the dig."

"That is something of an 'if' though," demurred Tania. "We do know that he did have beefs of his own with Malcolm, so I don't think we can cross him off the list at this stage. It's not as if the village is far away."

"Okay. So our list of potentials consist of the six, who all fell foul of Malcolm in some way or another. We have the other two men, Edward Wilton and Stephen Tisbury."

"Chalk and cheese as far as personality goes," remarked Tania.

"More chalk and cheese," continued Ron, "with the female members of the dig team. There's Victoria Whaddon, who's something of a delicate flower, and there's the robust Anne Langford, who I suspect couldn't see a goose without saying 'boo!' to it."

"Nicely put," laughed Tania. "And the last in the frame would be Mary Winterbourne, who had nothing at all to do with the excavations ..."

"But who would have had very much to do with the lead excavator if he'd had his unsavoury way," pointed out Ron. "So, there are our six characters in search of an accusing finger, if I may paraphrase the Pirandello play. And what do we know about them?"

"For a start, that each of them tells lies," responded Tania crisply. "Although actually," she swiftly corrected herself, "that isn't true. As far as we know, that is. Because as you said, Anne Langford was refreshingly robust in her assessment of Malcolm. She made no attempt to disguise her dislike of him, at least, not to us. To his face, she was doubtless less confrontational, although that seems not to have applied in both directions. But whether that directness of character translated into directness of action against him, we can't yet tell. Where do you hide a leaf? In a forest. Where do you hide a motive for murder? Amidst expressions of violent dislike for the victim?"

"And that, love, is an interesting psychological concept," said Ron, "but you did want to start with the basics, so simple soul that I am, I'd rather do that. And you did begin by saying that all the others tell lies, which is a plain fact. Each of them said, when we first started our series of friendly chats with them, that they had no issues with Malcolm, or that they admired his scholarship and work ethic or whatever, and it's only when we began to speak to other people that we discovered that these statements were, not to put too fine a point on it, a load of old guff. So, why are these people lying to us? Guilt?"

"It could be as simple as that. Although I'm pretty sure that we don't have a gigantic conspiracy along the lines of the Agatha Christie story where everyone is covering for everyone else because they're all responsible. No, I'm sure the reason is that nobody wants even a shadow of suspicion to fall on them, so they manipulate the truth to put themselves in a better light. It isn't malign. It's just human nature."

"Or else it's 'The dog ate my homework'," grinned Ron. "Because one of them is lying for the simple reason that they did actually do it. But I have to confess, I'm still scratching my head for a sufficient motive."

"True," reflected Tania. "It's mostly all harsh words. Sticks and stones. Although there are some practical potential hazards dotted amongst them."

"Such as?"

"Malcolm did pose a potential actual threat to both Stephen and Victoria's academic future. That could have had long-term repercussions. Ditto Edward. If Malcolm had sufficient influence, as it seems he must have done to get the position of expedition leader in the first place, a word from him in the right ear could have put a spoke in Edward's career. As for Mary, Anne, and George, they're more out of the direct firing line."

Ron reflected for a moment. "Here's a thought. I'm casting my mind back to the other cases we've been drawn into, and as well as threats to the various suspects, there's another common factor we haven't considered."

"And what's that?"

"Knowledge of a guilty secret. On top of being generally unpleasant to all and sundry, what if Malcolm had stumbled upon some piece of knowledge which presented a hazard to one of our people? Although I have no idea how he might have come by this knowledge. It's not as if any of them had crossed his path before."

"Are we absolutely certain of that?" queried Tania. "That hasn't come up in any of our conversations."

"Purely because the thought hadn't struck us before," responded Ron. "But maybe it's worth a second round of chats to verify, yes or no. And if yes, then we dig a little deeper."

Tania nodded. "That's one for tomorrow, I think. Because we did say that today would be a nice relaxing walk with these two lovable animals, immersing ourselves in the delights of nature and pushing all thoughts of murder from our minds." She laughed. "Not actually turning out that way so far, is it?"

"I blame George," said Ron. "If he hadn't stuck his head up over his garden wall, this conversation would never have started. And we've been so busy talking that I haven't been paying the slightest attention to where we've been and what we've seen. And I was hoping we might see that kingfisher again, but I dare say we've managed to scare him well away with our talking."

"No, actually," said Tania, looking ahead. "If I remember rightly, the pool where we saw him was a little further down, just past the bend in the path. So if we can manage to keep quiet, you may still be in with a chance."

The couple proceeded cautiously down through the shade alongside the stream in the tree-filled valley, accompanied by their naturally soft-footed companions, and seated themselves on a fallen tree. From the nearby undergrowth came the peremptory tick of a robin, while in the distance could be heard the faint drumming of a woodpecker.

"Plenty of bird-life around these woods," murmured Ron. "Just not the one we were hoping ..."

"Shhh!" Tania stilled her husband with a brisk command. She inclined her head silently in the direction of a bush on the far bank, as the brightly-coloured head of a bird emerged from a burrow in the overhang and flitted up into the foliage, before darting downstream and vanishing. "And that," she said, "could not have been better timed. It's almost as if he was waiting for us."

"And I'm not at all sure that he wasn't. I've always suspected that you, my love," said Ron fondly, "have magical powers. Probably why you were such a brilliant Queen of the Fairies when we did 'A Midsummer Night's Dream' in Cornwall."

"Matched only by you as my King," responded Tania with a kiss. "So, now that you've seen your kingfisher, I think it's time we found somewhere to have our picnic. All this talking has given me an appetite. Any suggestions?"

"'*I know a bank where the wild thyme blows*'," quoted Ron, provoking a smile from his wife. "I seem to remember a little grassy clearing a bit further on. We can tether the alpacas so that they can have a nibble while we eat." He stood and addressed the animals. "Come along, you two. Time for a bit of snap. But no cake!" he added sternly to Santiago. The little party went on their way, and were soon lost to sight amidst the trees.

Chapter 15

"Do you know what I think?" asked Ron, as he cleared the table after the couple's early evening meal.

"Very rarely, darling," smiled Tania, running water into the kitchen sink. "But that's what makes our marriage fun."

The pair had returned to the farm pleasantly exhausted after their lengthy trek with their animal companions, and after handing them back to Henry with assurances that the animals had behaved perfectly, and having received the comforting news that the little alpaca Rio's ills were nothing more than a minor digestive upset, Tania and Ron had agreed that a siesta was the order of the day. Both slept long and soundly, and it was with some surprise that they woke simultaneously to find that the afternoon was fast turning into evening. It was decided that an early supper was indicated after having had only a modest lunch, so Ron busied himself in the kitchen creating a paella from various items in the fridge. A welcome bottle of Rioja was discovered in a wine rack at the back of the larder. The talk over the meal was of inconsequential things - their good fortune with the weather, pleasantly warm for the time of year but not extreme - the fanciful shapes created by the clouds forming over a distant range of hills - *'The cloud-capped towers, the gorgeous palaces'* quoted Ron dreamily - or the pair of buzzards performing an aerial ballet high above a wheat field on the edge of the Downs as the couple were heading back towards the farm. But now, as he deposited the dishes in the hot water, Ron's brow furrowed in thought.

"Various people mentioned that the police had been back to the farm with questions while we were on our original walk with Henry and the alpacas," he pointed out. "But what we didn't ask was what those questions were. For all we know, they might have revealed some information about the murder which we aren't aware of."

"And also given us an insight into Inspector Copper's thinking," added Tania.

Ron chuckled. "After the case at the Abbey, I suspect that's the last thing he'd be wanting to share with you. He wasn't reluctant to issue his 'stay out of it' warning when we ran into him here on the morning after Malcolm's death, was he?"

"True," agreed Tania.

"Not that you will be paying the slightest attention to that warning," declared Ron. "It isn't in your nature."

"My first loyalty is to Leah," retorted Tania. "I want this case sorted out for her peace of mind. As well as everyone else's."

"We did speak about going round everyone for a second series of chats," said Ron. "And I suppose Leah is as good as any to begin with. And no time like the present. So you wash, I'll dry, and then we'll go and knock on her door."

*

"How as your walk?" enquired Leah, as the couple took their seats in the farmhouse sitting room. "Henry told me he'd entrusted two of his favourite animals into your tender care. Although I suspect he was slightly holding his breath until you came back safely with them."

"It was very relaxing," replied Ron.

"To an extent," added Tania. "That is, until the elephant in the room popped its head above the parapet once more. Really, it's impossible to forget why we're here, so we were turning over everything we knew about all the people potentially involved in Malcolm's death. And also wondering what it might be that we didn't know. And it occurred to Ron that we knew the police had been back carrying out further interviews with everyone, but we hadn't gone into what it was that they were asking. We thought you could help."

"Mostly it was a matter of alibis," stated Leah. "Of course, for me it was easy. I was nowhere near the farm at the time, and I'd given Inspector Constable Martha Talbot's phone number so that he could verify what I'd told him. Which I'm happy to say he'd already done. So there was nothing much more he could ask me, so he went on to the others with his main question."

"Which was?" prompted Ron.

"Obviously, where they were between midnight and one a.m.," responded Leah.

"Hah!" exclaimed Ron. "At last something concrete! We have a time of death."

"Oh. I thought you knew that." Leah sounded puzzled.

"How could we?" asked Tania. "We knew it was at some time during the night, but we had no more information than that. We saw the forensics people taking Malcolm away on Monday morning, but that's all. Evidently they've examined the body and come to a conclusion as to timing."

"And does that help?"

"It means we know what sort of questions to ask people," explained Tania. "And if I know anything about human nature, I'd guess that everyone was no more forthcoming about their whereabouts or activities at the relevant time than they were when we first spoke to them about their relationships with Malcolm. People don't like talking to the police, even if they've got nothing to hide."

"And you think you can get more out of them than the inspector?" Leah sounded dubious. "Because I am sure that the word has percolated that you two are not the innocent and harmless tourists you portrayed yourselves as."

"No," countered Tania, "but we are good friends of yours who are doing their best to solve a problem which is affecting you deeply. So with a bit of luck, we can coax some co-operation out of them."

"Well, good luck with that," said Leah grimly. "And I wouldn't mind betting that you're planning on being about it straight away. So my question is, would you like a wee dram to steady yourselves before you start?"

*

"I'm not absolutely convinced that I'm steadied," said Ron. "Leah's definition of a 'wee dram' is not exactly what I'd call wee. She does pour with a heavy hand."

"I'm sure you'll manage," replied Tania. "But it's true, she is a generous woman. But don't worry. If you start to slur your words, I'll give you a sharp nudge."

Ron came sharply to attention. "Guaranteed no slurring, ma'am. So, who do you want to begin with?"

"We started with the boss, so let's move on to the second-in-command. And if my memory serves me correctly, Mary Winterbourne lives in the Old Piggery ..." Tania pointed across the farmyard. "Which is just over there by her office in the Tack Room."

Mary answered the knock at her door with a faint air of surprise. "Hello Tania, Ron," she said. "What can I do for you?" But then her expression grew more reserved. "Or can I guess?"

"I expect you probably can," said Tania.

"You'd better come in then." Mary drew back from the doorway and ushered the couple into a comfortably-furnished sitting room, gesturing towards a sofa. She switched off the television and regarded her visitors warily. "I was just watching the local news. Of course, we feature. And I suspect that you've come calling on the same subject."

"What are they saying?" enquired Tania.

"Very little. There isn't really very much they can say. The police are obviously being tight-lipped."

"Would that be, I wonder, because people here

are being equally tight-lipped?" asked Tania. "We know they've been back questioning everybody."

"And no doubt you're planning on doing the same," said Mary resignedly. "Although what you hope to be able to do that the police can't, I can't imagine."

"Find some sort of crack in the story that will allow the truth to slip through," said Tania.

Ron took up the thread. "The thing is, we originally thought that everyone was providing an alibi for everyone else, because you were all together down at the pub on Saturday night and you all returned to the farm together. That's broadly true. But we now know, which we didn't before, that the police have narrowed the time of the murder down to between midnight and one in the morning. Lord knows how the forensics people managed to do it so precisely, but I'll take their word for it."

"It's probably something to do with stomach contents," surmised Tania. "If they know what Malcolm had consumed by way of a meal that evening, plus whatever drinks he had at the pub, they can deduce things from the rate of digestion as to the time of death."

"Thanks for drawing that picture for me, love," remarked Ron. "Too much information. However, if that's what the official conclusion is, I'm happy to go with that. So, Mary, I imagine that the inspector will have asked you if you could account for your movements at that time."

"And I'll tell you exactly what I told him," replied Mary. "I was here, alone, in bed and fast asleep. And no, there was nobody in bed with me able to verify that. Least of all Malcolm Sutherland," she added with a bitter twist to her mouth. "Although if he'd had his way, he'd probably still be with us instead of lying on a mortuary slab."

"Fair point," observed Tania drily. "And of course it would be ludicrous to suggest that he might have made some sort of attempt to, as you put it, 'have his way' after your return that evening, after which he could have gone up to the dig site for some unknown reason, with you following in his footsteps and putting a permanent end to any further advances."

Mary gave Tania a long level look. "As you say, ludicrous," she responded shortly.

"My wife's fondness for murder mystery literature sometimes tempts her into creating the most convoluted scenarios," said Ron with a smile intended to disarm. "But coming back to plain facts, there is one thing which I don't believe anyone has considered. Which is, had you met Malcolm Sutherland before he arrived here on the farm at the start of the excavations? Because if there were any sort of prior contact, that could be a factor in the police's investigations."

"And yours, of course," responded Mary. "But I can tell you plainly, I'd never clapped eyes on the man before he came here on that day."

"And presumably had very little to do with him while the dig was taking place up on the Downs?"

"As little as possible," was the sharp retort.

"Minimal contact, then?" confirmed Tania. "The dig, and some attempts to ... befriend you which came to nothing. Outside that, nothing?"

"Yes. Although ..."

Tania's attention sharpened. "Although what?"

"There was one day, early on, when I went into my office and found him going through the paperwork on my desk. I asked him what on earth he was up to, and he made some excuse about wondering how Leah's business was doing, and was I in charge of all the administration. I told him it was none of his business and practically threw him out."

"And did it go any further afterwards?"

"No. But I made sure that everything was securely locked away after that."

Tania got to her feet. "We won't take up any more

of your time. Sorry to have interrupted your evening."

"I know you're only trying to help sort things out for Leah's benefit," said Mary. "But just don't feel you have to look too hard to find Malcolm Sutherland's murderer. In my opinion, the world is better off without him."

*

"Who next?" asked Ron, as the couple emerged into the farmyard, but before Tania could answer, the were interrupted by the sudden appearance of Henry Gifford out of the gathering gloom of the evening.

"Hello, Henry," Tania greeted him. "I didn't expect to find you out and about at this hour."

"I ... er ... I just popped up to make sure that Rio is feeling all right," replied Henry. "I do that sometimes of an evening - check that the beasts are settled down for the night."

"Making sure they're all safely tucked up in bed, eh?" grinned Ron.

The colour rose in Henry's cheeks. "I like to take care of them," he said gruffly.

"What a shame you didn't do that on the night Professor Sutherland was killed," said Tania. "You might have seen something. But of course, you were back at the pub with Jane when the whole party left."

"I was that," agreed Henry.

"I know the police have been around asking when everyone last saw the professor, and where they were at the crucial time of death."

"Oh, they've asked me that too," said Henry. "I just repeated what I'd already told them. Mind you, there was one thing that slipped my mind."

Tania's attention sharpened. "And what was that?"

"I don't suppose it's important. It's just that, as everyone was leaving the pub, I heard George say 'I'm sure there was something. I could help. I could bring my metal detector back up', and the professor said 'Leave it!', sharply-like. 'I'm not having that thing on my site again. This is my dig'. But he seemed edgy or excited for some reason. Lord knows why. And then off they went."

"We'll have a chat with George. See if he can shed any light," said Tania. "Back to the pub now, is it?"

"Well, I do need to check whether Jane needs any help behind the bar," said Henry with something like a conspiratorial smile, as he made his way out of the yard.

*

"Now, where were we?" asked Ron.

"On our way to ask some questions," said Tania. "So how about paying the gentlemen a visit?" She made a beeline across the yard to Henge Cottage and rapped on the door.

The knock was answered by Edward Wilton, who emitted a sigh of resignation when he realised who the callers were. "Ah. Mr and Mrs Faye, come to pursue your enquiries into my predecessor's death, no doubt."

"Good evening, Mr Wilton," replied Tania, slightly taken aback by the manner of their welcome. "Actually, we would be glad of a word, if you can spare a moment."

"You'd better come in," said Edward with some reluctance, and the three were soon seated somewhat awkwardly in the cottage's sitting room.   "I take it you've abandoned the pretence of being coincidental arrivals on the scene," he remarked. "After a brief comparison of notes with my colleagues, it's clear what you're about."

"We ought to apologise for our deception," responded Tania. "But it was all in a good cause. We are truly long-standing friends of Leah's, and it was in response to an appeal from her that we arrived here. She had some idea that our previous brushes with sudden death might give me some sort of insight into what happened with Malcolm Sutherland. She had faith that I might discover facts which had eluded the official police investigation."

"Yes, I understand that you are regarded as some sort of local sleuth. So, have you made any discoveries?" challenged Edward.

"Possibly," said Tania. "But there are many things we still don't know. For instance, we only found out today that the time of the murder has been established as between midnight and one a.m., and it seems helpful to know where people were at that time."

"Or say they were," put in Ron.

"And you're asking me the same question," stated Edward. "Fine. I have nothing to hide. I was, if you must know, sat up burning the midnight oil compiling a report. I believed it might be helpful. I will admit, there had been some, shall I say, strained circumstances between my predecessor and myself, so I had decided to write a detailed account of proceedings at the dig for the authorities at Camford. I did so on the Saturday at the end of each week. For the avoidance of any misunderstandings as to what had occurred and what finds had been made, you understand."

Tania nodded. "I think I do. Perhaps something to do with the attribution of discoveries."

"Quite." A grim smile from the professor.

"And I hope this can all be confirmed by your companion in the cottage," said Tania.

"Probably not," replied Edward. "Stephen disappeared into his room as soon as we returned that evening, muttering something about checking up on his social media. And I started down here, but then I went up to my own room shortly afterwards and settled down at the desk with my laptop. At the end of which, I went to bed, but I couldn't tell you exactly what time that was. Certainly after twelve."

"So neither you nor Stephen could confirm each other's presence? You didn't, for instance, hear him leave his room?"

"I don't keep my ear pressed to the door listening for other people's movements," retorted Edward in a waspish tone. "I was far too busy concentrating on what I was writing."

"And the last time you saw Professor Sutherland would have been when the group returned from the Drover's Rest?" enquired Ron.

"Yes," insisted Edward firmly. "And to be frank, I am sick of repeating the fact."

"Then I think we'd better leave it at that," said Tania, getting to her feet. "But I wonder if it might be possible to have a word with Stephen before we go. He may have something to contribute. Because you never know ... That's if he's here."

Another sigh from Edward. "Of course. And he's up in his room. As usual. We don't normally socialise a great deal. So it's top of the stairs, and the first door on the right."

"Thank you, Professor." Tania and Ron headed for the foot of the staircase out in the hall, and the sitting room door was closed firmly behind them.

Chapter 16

Tania tapped gently at the door at the head of the stairs. No response. She tapped again, with a similar result.

"Let me," said Ron, and knocked more robustly on the bedroom door, but still without success. "Oh, this is ridiculous!" he fumed. "Has the stupid boy done a runner or something?" He threw open the door.

The figure lying on the bed leapt like a panicked rabbit, and fumbled to pull the earbuds from his ears. "What ...?" he gasped.

"Sorry to burst in," said Ron in brusque apology, "but we did knock. Three times, actually."

"I didn't hear," replied Stephen, struggling into a sitting position and setting aside his laptop. "I was streaming some music. Mahler, actually. There's nothing much else to do around here in the evenings," he added disconsolately.

"You could be socialising with your friends from the excavation," suggested Tania.

"They're not exactly my friends," said Stephen. "It's not as if we're the same generation. Edward's more like my dad."

"What about Victoria?" enquired Tania with a twinkle. "She's the same sort of age as you."

Stephen coloured. "But she's ... I mean, she's never ... Anyway, I don't think she'd be interested." His shoulders slumped.

"Anyway, we're not here to discuss anyone's social life," intervened Ron, taking pity on the young man.

"So what do you want?"

"Do you mind if we come in?" asked Tania. "We just wanted a chat about a few things."

"Why not?" shrugged Stephen, moving aside to allow Tania to perch on the end of the bed, while Ron took a seat in the upright chair at the small desk in the corner of the room.

"You're probably aware that my husband and I are looking into this matter of Malcolm Sutherland's killing," began Tania. "Leah, the lady who owns the farm, asked us to, alongside the police investigation. We're old friends, and she hoped that we might uncover something that others could have missed."

"Oh," said Stephen, clearly perplexed. "But why ..."

"So we're talking to everyone again," pressed on Tania, "in the light of the fresh information that's emerged today, namely the likely time of death. And everyone's been very helpful in confirming where they were at that time, and I was hoping you might be able to do the same."

"What time are you talking about?" asked Stephen. "Is it the same time as the police asked me about? Because if so, I've already told them everything."

"And that would be ...?" invited Tania.

Stephen huffed with slight impatience. "I was up here in my room. As I said to the inspector," he continued with a note of resentment. "Everyone came back from the pub, and I came straight up here because I'd had enough of hanging around people trying to make polite conversation. So I had a shower, got into bed, and then I put my music on."

"More Mahler?" asked Ron.

"Lady Gaga, actually."

"And probably with your earphones in, and quite loudly, just like it must have been when we came knocking," smiled Ron. "So I'm guessing you wouldn't have heard anything other than that. You wouldn't, for instance, have heard Professor Wilton moving about?"

Stephen shook his head. "Not a thing. I left him downstairs writing something or other. And I suppose he must have come up to his room at some point because he came out of there the next morning as I was going downstairs, but I've no idea when."

"And you didn't leave the room again at any point?" Ron sought to confirm.

"No. I'm not like one of those old blokes," added Stephen with a faint sneer, "who have to get up six times in the night."

"Good to know," said Tania lightly. "So, the other thing we're confirming is when people saw Professor Sutherland for the last time. And we've been told by everyone else that that would have been when you all returned to the farm on Saturday evening after leaving the pub. I imagine that it would be the same for you?"

"Actually, no," was Stephen's unexpected response.

"Oh?" Tania leaned forward. "So what can you tell us that's different?"

"I'd finished listening to the concert," explained Stephen, "and I couldn't be bothered to start streaming anything else, so I got out of bed to put my laptop back on the desk. And I just glanced out of the window, and I saw somebody out in the farmyard near the gate to the path up to the dig. It's quite dark out there, and at the time I thought it must be the chap who looks after the animals, come to check up on something, but thinking about it, it was too tall for him. I think it could have been the professor. But when I looked again a minute later, I couldn't see anyone. Just a flickering light."

*

"That's a turn-up for the books," remarked Ron, as the couple stood once more in the farmyard. "What on earth was Malcolm up to out here in the yard at midnight?"

"We know what," retorted Tania. "Obviously that was when he was on his way to the dig site. But the question remains, why? What was he hoping to achieve once he got there? Some sort of discovery? But what or who? And why in the middle of the night?"

Ron shrugged. "I'm no wiser than you. But one

thing we can probably be sure of. It wouldn't have been Stephen. I can't see him going off to some midnight rendezvous with Malcolm after the way he'd been treated."

"Unless, that is," reflected Tania, "he'd somehow been coerced into doing so. Wild flight of fancy, I know, but suppose Malcolm discovered that he had cheated on his exams to get into Camford, for instance, and was threatening to expose him ..."

"So to speak," interjected Ron.

Tania gave him a look before continuing. "... unless he fell in with Malcolm's unsavoury demands. And it all became too much, so Stephen put an end to the threats in the most extreme way." She paused. "But that makes no sense. Why would Stephen volunteer having seen Malcolm if he didn't have to?"

"Suggestion," said Ron. "Stick a pin in it and move on. We've still got the two ladies to speak to, and it's getting no earlier. The prospect of Anne Langford answering the door in curlers and a nightie is one I don't relish."

"Are you living in the nineteen-fifties?" laughed Tania. "But you're right. Off to their cottage we go."

Ron's fears were not realised, as Anne Langford answered the door of Tumulus Cottage fully dressed, with glasses pushed up on to her forehead and a newspaper in her hand. "Thank goodness," she smiled unexpectedly, beckoning her visitors inside. "A distraction! There's rubbish on the television, Victoria has vanished to her room like a moody teenager, and this crossword is driving me insane. So a bit of company is precisely what I need."

"It's not exactly a social call, I'm afraid," apologised Tania. "To tell you the absolute truth, we're still on the hunt for extra information relating to Malcolm Sutherland's murder."

"This calls for refreshment," said Anne. "And

since I haven't quite managed to polish off that bottle of whisky of mine, despite many temptations, including this blasted crossword, I'm sure I can persuade you to join me." On receipt of enthusiastic agreement, particularly from Ron, Anne busied herself with bottle and glasses, before seating herself once more and regarding Tania with expectation. "So, you're following in the footsteps of Inspector Copper, who came calling again with further questions. Particularly about everyone's whereabouts in the wee small hours of Sunday morning."

"That's right," said Ron, between appreciative sips of his drink. "What we hadn't known before was the estimated time of death, which we gather he very helpfully revealed. So now we're seeing if we can wheedle any further snippets out of everyone which may not have emerged during the police questioning."

Anne frowned in thought. "I can't think of anything that I haven't already told the inspector. We came back from the pub fairly late, right on their closing time, and Victoria vanished to her room quite promptly, as she usually does. I suspect that the lure of social media, keeping up with her friends at uni, is too much for her to resist. I stayed down here for a while listening to some music on the radio. Once again, the television was utter rubbish, of course. And then I went to bed. Somewhere approaching twelve, I think."

"You didn't encounter Professor Sutherland after the party split up on your return from the village?" queried Tania.

"I'm delighted to say I did not," responded Anne. "The last thing I needed was him turning up on the doorstep. Although I suspect that such a thing may not have been a million miles from his mind with regard to a certain other lady."

"You know about that then?"

"Being neither blind nor deaf," smiled Anne. "Fortunately I had no such problems. Too long in the tooth, I dare say. So my last 'encounter', as you put it, was after getting back from the pub." A pause. "Although not my first."

Ron's interest was piqued. "Are you saying you knew Professor Sutherland beforehand?"

Anne smiled grimly. "I wouldn't say 'knew'. 'Bumped into' would be more accurate."

"How so?"

"It was at Camford, well before we came up here. It must have been while the arrangements for the expedition were in hand, and Professor Sutherland was obviously there to make plans. Anyway, I was heading through a door one way, and he was coming in the opposite direction, and he just barged through with a muttered 'Oh for goodness sake, get out of my way, woman', and marched off without a backward glance. Charming, I thought. Of course, I had no idea who he was then."

"Hardly the behaviour of a gentleman," nodded Tania.

"As you say. And going back to your previous question, the last I saw of the 'gentleman' was when I came indoors on Saturday night."

"And stayed indoors, I assume," said Tania. "I'm guessing Victoria would be able to vouch for that."

Anne regarded her sharply. "Unfortunately not. I didn't clap eyes on her any more that evening, nor she me. So if you're after confirmation of my alibi, I'm afraid you're out of luck."

"A shame," said Tania. "But I imagine it would probably have been difficult for either of you to have left the cottage without the other being aware of it."

"I'm afraid your imagination is letting you down," replied Anne drily. "I'm a light sleeper, so I wear earplugs. Very efficient ones, I may add. So Victoria could have left the premises accompanied by a brass band for all I know. Although why, goodness knows. But I wouldn't have heard a thing."

"We shall just have to ask her," said Tania lightly, getting to her feet. "Thank you for the drink. And Victoria's room - just up the stairs, is it?"

*

Victoria answered the knock at her bedroom door with the air of a timorous faun. "Oh. I thought it was Anne." She caught her breath. "Is something the matter?" she asked nervously.

"Not in the least." Tania's reply was warm and reassuring. "Everything's fine. Actually, we've just been having a chat with Anne downstairs, and she mentioned that you were up here, so we thought we'd take the opportunity of doing the same with you."

"Why? What about?" Victoria continued to cling to the door-post for support.

"Would you mind awfully if we came in?" said Tania. "We'd just like a brief word, and I'm sure we'd all be more comfortable inside than squashed out here on the landing."

"Oh. All right." Victoria turned and headed for a small armchair in one corner of the room, leaving the other two to make their way inside and seat themselves on the end of the bed. "So, what was it you wanted?" Victoria drew her legs up underneath her and clutched a cushion to herself, almost like a shield.

"Just a couple of things," said Tania in a disarming tone, "and probably nothing you haven't already told the police. They came calling again today, I believe."

"Yes," replied Victoria. "I was busy making some notes about Beowulf ..." She blushed. "Sorry, I mean the young warrior. I was leaning over his skull, checking again to see if there was any evidence of trauma or injury, and when I looked up, that police inspector was standing right in front of me. It made me jump."

"That young warrior's quite a favourite of yours, isn't he?" enquired Tania. "Do you find yourself imagining what he was like in life?"

"I know it 's silly." The blush returned.

"Good-looking and brave, I expect," remarked Ron. "Especially with that torc thing you were telling us about. And who knows, when you get to examining the body in the main chamber of the tomb, things might get even more exciting. That's if it does turn out to be a chieftain or some such. He'd be of even higher status. Maybe there's more jewellery to be found."

"That's what George said," replied Victoria. "I was talking to him about Beo ... about the young man, and he said that if he'd been allowed to use his metal detector earlier, all sorts of things might have appeared. But Professor Sutherland had banned it."

"Yes, we heard that something of the sort was said on Saturday night," said Tania.

"Contrary to proper archaeological procedures, apparently. Amateurish, the professor called it. I think he was just jealous that George was the first to get an indication about the bronze torc."

"Actually, it was about Saturday night that we wanted a word," said Tania. "We're just interested to know when it was that everybody last saw the professor. And I dare say you've already passed your recollections on to the police."

"I have," confirmed Victoria, now sounding more confident. "We all came back up to the farm together, and then split up when we got here."

"Do you by chance remember who was with whom during your return?" asked Ron.

Victoria screwed up her brow with the effort of memory. "I know the professor was out in front. I didn't mind that. And then George went into his own house, and that left just the four of us. I think Anne was talking with Professor Wilton, and I was just behind them, and then Stephen came and sort of attached himself to me. Not that we spoke much. Why? Does it matter?"

"Just trying to get a clear picture in my mind," smiled Ron blandly. "So then when you got back here, that would have been the last time you saw Professor Sutherland. But not again after that?"

"No. He disappeared round the corner to his apartment, and that was it. And the others went off to their own places, and Anne and I came back in here. She stayed downstairs and I came up here, and that was it."

"Did you go straight to bed?" asked Tania.

"No. Well, yes. I got into bed, but I was talking to my friends for a while."

"You phoned some friends?"

"No." Victoria's smile was faintly pitying. "I was in a group of my friends from uni on InstaChat."

"I see. Were you on for long?"

Victoria shrugged. "I'm not sure. Maybe an hour. And I went to sleep after that."

"You didn't go out again? And you didn't by any chance look out of the window at any point? Or happen to hear Anne moving about? After all, it must be very quiet around the farm at night."

"Too quiet for me. It's a bit creepy," said Victoria with a slight shudder. "But no, I didn't hear a thing. But I wouldn't anyway, because I had my phone playing music when I turned the light out. Just quietly. But it helps me to sleep."

*

"I don't think any of that told us anything we didn't already know," remarked Ron after the couple had let themselves out of Anne and Victoria's cottage.

"Only that absolutely nobody is able to provide a cast-iron alibi for anyone else," replied Tania.

"Are we actually getting anywhere?" wondered Ron. "It seems like all brick walls."

"Nothing of the sort," countered Tania. "In fact, we've learnt one very important thing, which is that Stephen saw a figure, who surely must have been

Professor Sutherland, out in the farmyard after everybody had presumably settled down for the night. That was around midnight. We know the professor went up to the barrow during the night, so that looks as if it was him setting out, because it chimes with the time of death that the police have got from Forensics. Question - who else, apart from Stephen, was aware of the fact? Everybody else says not. Somebody's lying. And still unresolved is the question of what the professor was intending by his midnight jaunt."

"And I still haven't a clue as to what that might be. And in fact, my brain is beginning to hurt."

"I have a potential cure for that," laughed Tania.

"An early night?" Ron's eyebrows rose hopefully.

"Not exactly," smiled his wife. "I was thinking more in terms of a medicinal pint down at the Drover's. That should relax you."

"Bit of a second best," grinned Ron, "but I'll take what I can get. Let me grab my wallet, and we'll head down."

Chapter 17

"Well, if it isn't our newest local celebrities," came the cheery greeting from behind the bar.

"You what?" responded Ron, startled.

"Oh, don't mind me," laughed Jane Sherrington. "Just my little joke. But the thing is, you can't help it in a village like this. Word gets around. Oh, don't look at me," she added hastily. "I'm not one to gossip, for all everybody expects me to, being the barmaid here. But it's not exactly the talk of the village, but the fact is that everyone seems to know what you're about." She dropped her voice theatrically. "The murder, I mean."

Ron cast a look over his shoulder, to find that all the other occupants of the bar seemed to be looking at him and Tania with varying degrees of open or covert curiosity. "And I suppose that the fact that you clean for several of the villagers wouldn't have anything to do with it," he remarked.

"Absolutely not," declared Jane stoutly. "Cross my heart." She lowered her voice once more. "Mind you, I can't answer for Billy, but don't quote me."

"So much for the seal of the landlord's confessional," murmured Tania to Ron. "However," she said, "we haven't come investigating tonight. We've had quite enough of that this evening - so much so that Ron says he is in danger of dying of thirst, and the situation can only be remedied by the application of a pint of Drover's Draught."

"And a G and T for Tania, please," added Ron, producing his wallet. "A large one."

"Coming right up."

"So," said Tania, perching on a bar stool as the drinks were placed in front of the couple, "what is the gossip around the village? Because even if you're not adding to it, which I totally believe," she said hurriedly as Jane seemed about to draw breath to bristle, "you must hear what people are thinking when you're in their houses dusting or whatever."

"Nobody has a clue. That's because nobody really knows the people up there, because all they've seen of them is when they've come in here, and then they've mostly stuck with themselves. The latest mad theory is that it was done by some international gang of treasure hunters who'd come to rob the tomb of all its gold and jewels, and the professor got in the way. Daft or what?" chuckled Jane. "In fact, the only one who hasn't joined in with the daftness is George Cheverell. He says any talk of treasure is ridiculous, because they haven't found anything of the sort so far. And he'd know, wouldn't he, with that little museum of his. Which I am never allowed anywhere near with my duster." She glanced across the bar. "In fact, you could ask him if you like. He's sat over there in the corner."

Tania looked across to where George was sat alone nursing a beer. "Good idea. We will in a second, but I just wanted to confirm something with you first. It's about Saturday night. We know that you and Henry practically had to push the dig people out of the bar at the end of the evening. And that would have been the last time you both saw Professor Sutherland."

"That's right," nodded Jane. "And then we had a late supper with Billy and his boys."

"So I understand. And you didn't leave the pub after that, either of you?"

"No."

"Particularly not Henry?"

"Now it's funny you should ask that," said Jane, "because he did think of popping up to the farm after supper. Said he had a strange feeling that something might be up with the animals, but I told him not to be so daft, and they were perfectly all right when he left them earlier on, so he never went in the end."

"That's helpful," mused Tania.

"Why's that?" wondered Jane.

"Oh, nothing," said Ron airily. "Just confirming what Ste... - what one of the others said."

"So shall we take Jane's advice and go and have a word with George, darling?" suggested Tania, with a meaningful quirk to an eyebrow. "I'm sure Jane's got lots she should be getting on with instead of gossiping ... that is, instead of talking with us."

"Good idea, love." Ron picked up the drinks and headed over to the corner booth where George Cheverell was ensconced. "Good evening, George," he greeted him. "Mind if we join you?"

George came out of a reverie with a slight start. "Oh, hello. No, of course. Do sit down."

Tania and Ron installed themselves on the opposite side of the booth. "How are things going up at the excavation?" began Tania. "We haven't had a chance to chat with you since Monday, and I'm sure there must have been lots of developments since then."

"A few," smiled George. "The skeleton of the main figure is emerging. Victoria is probably getting quite excited to begin examining the bones."

"Any ideas as to who it may be yet?" enquired Ron.

"Not so far. There are some grave goods to analyse, but Professor Wilton is holding back from making any early judgements. Investigations are on-going, he says."

"No great treasures?" smiled Ron.

He was rewarded with a tight smile from George. "I think ideas like that are being discouraged."

"Shame," said Tania lightly. "Well, we shall just have to wait and see."

"And on the subject of investigations, I wonder how your own is getting on," said George.

"Ah. You're aware of the village gossip regarding our activities," replied Tania. "Well, I have to say I'm sorry if we misled you at the start, but we were trying to be discreet for Leah's benefit."

"Hmmm," was George's response.

"But since you ask," continued Tania, "we're just confirming with people when they last saw Professor Sutherland. And in your case, we understand it would have been when the party left here on Saturday night, or rather, when you left the party to go into your house, leaving the rest to carry on up towards the farm."

"And that's correct. Why, does somebody say different?"

"No, not at all. Now I hope you won't be offended when I say this," ventured Tania, "but I don't think you were one hundred percent accurate when you told us initially about how you viewed Professor Sutherland."

"I don't know what you mean," responded George warily.

"Oh, you're not alone," interjected Ron. "Almost everyone gave us a slightly edited version of their opinion of him to begin with. Not wishing to speak ill of the dead, I expect."

George sighed. "I did actually try to make friends with him at the start. I thought I'd be able to learn a lot from him, with him having such a reputation and being so knowledgeable. At least, that's what the high-ups at Camford said when he was appointed as head of the expedition, or so I gather from the others. And in fact I even persuaded him to come in and take a look at my little exhibition at home."

"Oh yes? How did that come about?" wondered Ron.

"It was in the very early days. We'd all had hardly a chance to get to know one another, and we'd come down here to the Drover's for a lunchtime drink. It was actually Anne's suggestion. I think she saw herself as a sort of general auntie combined with social secretary of the group. Sadly it didn't quite work. Professor

Sutherland didn't really seem in the mood. But as we were coming away and heading back to the farm, I mentioned my museum to the professor and invited him in to see it as we were passing my cottage."

"I imagine he would have been quite impressed with your enthusiasm," said Tania. "And your display."

George's face set. "Not so much. In fact, he was quite dismissive. Described my display as a worthless collection of refuse."

Tania was surprised. "What, even that prize exhibit of yours? That little silver coin that started you off?"

George pulled a face. "That worst of all. He said it was a good thing it was only silver. If it had been gold, he would have felt compelled to report me to the authorities for breaking the law about declaring finds."

"Not what you'd want to hear," remarked Ron. "I bet you're relieved you never found any gold up at this dig of yours, or else Professor Sutherland would have had the police down on you like a ton of bricks," he added, chuckling.

George's face took on an expression of longing. "Yes. Something gold would have been wonderful." His eyes sparkled. "But you know we've only got the bronze torc so far."

"But with hopes of finding other things," said Tania. "Because you offered to use your metal detector to help examine the main chamber, didn't you?"

"Who told you that?"

"Just something we heard. It was on the last evening, wasn't it? The night the professor was killed."

"Well, I never got to do so, did I?" said George. "And now Professor Wilton is in charge, and he wants to be more traditional in his methods."

"I'm sure they'll bring the results you all want," said Tania reassuringly. "I just wish Ron and I could say the same." She finished her drink and stood. "We'd better not impose on George any more, darling."

"Right," said Ron, gulping down the remains of his pint. "Off we go then."

As the couple were making their way towards the exit, they were hailed by Billy Charlton from behind the bar. "Not leaving so soon, you two? Plenty of drinking time left this evening," he smiled.

"I know Ron would probably love to," replied Tania, "but I've got so many things turning over in my mind that I feel in need of a little quiet thinking time."

"Still on the case, eh? All Jessica Fletcher, is it?" chuckled Billy. "Well, don't go just yet. Sit yourselves down here, and let me give you a drink on the house, while I share a snippet or two with you."

"Now that's an offer no sensible sleuth would turn down," grinned Ron, hoisting himself on to a bar stool.

"They say the pub landlord knows all there is to know," smiled Tania in response. She took a seat alongside her husband. "So, Billy, if you insist."

"I do," said Billy. "Same again?" The drinks were produced, and Billy leaned forward to rest his arms on the bar. "I see you've been having a chat with our George. What did he have to say for himself?"

"He was telling us about showing his collection of finds to Professor Sutherland in the early days of the dig," said Tania. "Apparently it didn't go well."

"I can't say I'm surprised," said Billy, "having heard what that professor had to say about him. I reckon it's pulled his horns in a bit. He's usually pretty social when he comes in here of an evening, but he's gone a bit quiet. Probably the effect of being so close to a murder. I dare say it's affected the whole lot of them up there."

"Thinking about it, you're probably right," agreed Ron. "We've been talking to all of them, and they're all affected in one way or another. Some of them not exactly consumed by grief at Sutherland's death," he added with a grin. "Anne Langford was particularly robust in her opinions."

"From what I've seen of her, I imagine she would be. Woman of a certain age, you see. She's seen a bit of life, so she knows what's what. And not likely to put up with any nonsense."

"I think it would be fair to say the same about Mary Winterbourne," said Tania. "Although it's difficult to tell whether she'd be more relieved that Malcolm Sutherland wasn't in a position to make himself an unwanted nuisance, or more worried about the effect the whole murder situation was having on the business of the farm. And of course, then there's Leah. All right, she was long separated from Malcolm, but she obviously had feelings for him once, so you'd think there would be at least the dregs of sadness that he's dead. Thank goodness it's proved beyond doubt that she was miles away at the time of the murder and couldn't possibly have had anything to do with it."

"She's the lucky one," remarked Billy. "Shame the youngsters can't say the same. Specially that Stephen boy. Now I'm not one to point fingers, and I haven't told the police all I know, because if they don't ask the right questions, they won't get the right answers." He took a deep breath. "However, if I'd been in that lad's position, given what I overheard that time in the back corridor - you remember I told you about that - I reckon the cops would be looking at him long and hard."

"He seems to be another one who's retreated somewhat from the world," observed Tania. "But I couldn't tell you whether that's some sort of manifestation of guilt or just a result of the whole unsettling situation."

"Cos he's one who hasn't had the experience of life," nodded Billy. "Ain't had the opportunity to build up his reserves of strength. I wouldn't mind betting that young girl's the same. Victoria, isn't it?"

"That's right," said Ron. "Actually, I feel a little sorry for her. When we were first here and we went to see the finds she was examining in the old barn, she was very enthusiastic about everything, but then to have had Professor Sutherland dismissing her efforts in what sounded like quite a threatening way must have dented her confidence. And then there's the added complication that Stephen is smitten with her and seems to follow her around like a puppy, and I'm not sure she knows how to handle that gracefully in the midst of all the emotional turmoil of a murder case."

"And I'm not sure how Professor Wilton knows quite how to handle himself either," observed Tania. "On one hand he's now in charge of the expedition, which I assume is exactly what he would have wanted in the first place, so you'd think he'd be as pleased as a dog with two tails. But against that, of course, there's the assumption that he'd be full of resentment at the bringing in of Professor Sutherland over his head, so he's obviously jumpy in case the police believe that there is a good and sufficient motive for murder in that."

"Seems to me," said Billy, "that the only one who wasn't suffering during the whole period of the dig was Professor Sutherland himself."

"With the exception of the eventual outcome," pointed out Ron drily.

"I wonder," mused Tania. "He was obviously very much in control on the surface. But you wonder how good a man like that was at handling rejection. For one thing, there was Mary Winterbourne stating baldly that she'd have nothing to do with him, and for another, we're going to have to deduce from what you observed, Billy, that something comparable happened with Stephen. Being rejected isn't a comfortable experience. Maybe Leah can shed some light on how Malcolm handled the matter in the light of their break-up."

"And perhaps it could be a factor in making him

so unpleasant to the others," said Ron. "Could it have made him over-compensate when it came to passing judgement on the other members of his dig team. We've heard how dismissive he was of Victoria and Anne, not to mention Professor Wilton. You'd have thought that he'd be full of confidence at having been brought in over Mr Wilton's head, but was he? I wonder. And we've already heard from George this evening, confirming what we'd been told by other people, that Malcolm had very little time for him. Professional standards, do we think, or something like a deep-seated uncertainty about his own worth?"

"And none of this explains why Malcolm would be heading up to the barrow in the dead of night," sighed Tania. "To meet someone? It seems very unlikely, unless Stephen or Mary had a total change of heart, which sounds absurd. To talk progress or discuss plans with Professor Wilton? Again, why in the middle of the night? It isn't plausible. But there was something that drew him up there. But what?"

"I couldn't tell you that, my dear," said Billy, "but there was one thing I did notice. When the group was all leaving here, Jane and Henry were almost having to crowbar them out of the door, but I did catch sight of the expression on Professor Sutherland's face, just for a moment, and he did seem to have a sort of gleam in his eye. Don't ask me why. It just struck me as a bit odd. Almost as odd as him standing everybody else a round of drinks earlier in the evening, which I'd not known him do before."

"Actually," said Tania, "that confirms something that Henry mentioned to us about the same thing. When the group was leaving, I mean. And he said that, for some reason, the professor seemed excited about something. So that must have been what drew him up to the Downs for his clandestine visit to the barrow. One of them must hold the key to this. But which one?"

Chapter 18

As Tania sat in bed sipping her early morning tea, she was surprised to see the flash of blue lights playing on the buildings of the farmyard. "Looks as if the police are back," she remarked.

Ron looked at his watch. "At this hour? It's barely eight o'clock. What on earth brings them back up here at the crack of dawn?"

"Hardly that, darling," laughed Tania. "Just because we're having a little holiday, it doesn't mean that the forces of law and order aren't still hard at work. But obviously something's afoot to bring them here this early."

"Well, I don't propose to bound forth instantly in order to find out," replied Ron. "I need my second cup, plus a refreshing shower, plus a hearty breakfast. By which time Leah may know what's going on."

"Sounds like a plan," agreed Tania. "And speaking of second cups, the tide seems to have gone out in mine."

*

As Tania and Ron emerged from their cottage some while later, they were in time to see Sergeant Radley shepherding all the members of the archaeological group into the finds barn, with Inspector Copper standing on one side observing the proceedings. The two overall-clad officers from the forensics team could be seen placing a plastic bag into the rear of their van, before the pair of women followed the others into the barn.

"I wonder what on earth is going on," said Ron.

"I wish somebody would tell me," said Leah, who had appeared unobserved behind the couple. "All I know is that the police turned up unannounced an hour ago, wanting to know who was staying where, and saying that all the dig people were to stay put in their cottages for the time being. And that included Mary. And when

George arrived, he sent him in to join her. They then disappeared up to the site, including those two women in the white suits. I can only assume that they have been looking for something up there."

"They must think they've missed something first time around," deduced Tania. "And that plastic bag presumably contains some sort of evidence."

"And then they came back down just now," continued Leah, "and went around hauling people out of their houses and sending them into the hay-barn. I can't think what they're up to."

"I can tell you what they're up to," declared Mary Winterbourne, who had just emerged from the barn and come striding across the farmyard to where the others were standing. "They are busily taking DNA samples from all of us. Those nasty little swabs from the inside of the cheeks."

"So what's that all about?" wondered Ron.

"Maybe they've ideas about the murder weapon," speculated Tania. "DNA traces on something, perhaps. I wonder what's in that bag."

"I haven't got time to stand here wondering," said Mary brusquely. "I have work to get on with, even if nobody else has. Somebody has to try to keep the administration of this place on an even keel if we're not to go under completely."

"Are things so bad?" asked Leah, concerned.

Mary huffed. "Oh, I dare say we'll get through, just as soon as everything's sorted out and the police leave us alone. I need to do a push on social media, even though personally I dislike them intensely."

"Why don't you get Henry to help you?" suggested Leah, as the alpaca handler appeared at the entrance to the yard, seeming nonplussed at the unusual activity. "He has a lot to do with the children when they come for walks. Maybe he'll have some ideas on how to appeal to them, and they can persuade their parents to forget the news stories and think about how lovable the animals are."

"It's a thought," said Mary grudgingly. "Henry!" she called. "I need you. Come with me, and I'll tell you what's going on." She headed into the Tack Room with a puzzled-looking Henry in her wake.

Tania, Ron and Leah stood watching as, one by one, the excavation team emerged from the hay-barn to join Edward Wilton, first to appear after Mary, in the corner of the farmyard next to the gate giving on the path to the dig. After a murmured conference, everyone disappeared back into their respective cottages, before returning moments later and heading through the gate and up towards the barrow. And just after that, Inspector Copper and his sergeant exited the barn, followed by the two forensics officers who made a beeline for their van.

As the inspector bore down on Leah, Tania attempted to sidle unobtrusively in the direction of the women who were loading their equipment into the rear doors of their vehicle. "You're the forensics people, aren't you?" she addressed the leading officer brightly. "I hope you managed to find something useful,"

The woman turned to her with a wry expression. "Ah. You must be Mrs Faye," she smiled. "I've heard all about you from my husb... from the inspector. And I gather that you have a fascination for all things to do with this case, but I'm sure you know as well as I do that I couldn't possibly divulge any details."

"I wouldn't expect you to for a moment," replied Tania with an answering smile. "Although I'd love to know if you've managed yet to get a handle on the murder." The officer shot her an odd look, but did not speak.. "But you can't expect me not to be curious," continued Tania, peering into the van's interior. "For example, that plastic bag looks fascinating. And the contents appear to be ... what, a pair of surgical gloves? Rather like the ones you've just taken off? Except that they look a bit dirty. Of course, it's not easy to see through the plastic."

"I don't think Sergeant Singleton is planning on discussing her work with you, Mrs Faye," came the voice of Inspector Copper at her shoulder. He reached past her and slammed the doors of the van. "Neither am I. And I've just told Mrs Sutherland that, for the moment, she and her staff, as well as the team of archaeologists, are free to continue their own work. All, I hope, without any interference from third parties."

"Inspector, what do you take me for?" laughed Tania. "I'd be the last person to prevent you from solving your case."

"Hmmm," grunted Copper. Without a further word, he gestured to his sergeant, and the police party climbed into their respective vehicles and headed out of the farmyard.

"Learn anything?" enquired Ron as his wife rejoined him, Leah having disappeared into the Tack Room in the footsteps of Mary and Henry.

"Not a huge amount," confessed Tania. "That forensics officer was not exactly handing out the information."

"Tight as a duck's proverbial, eh?" chuckled Ron.

"But I have two snippets, one of which obviously relates to the case, and the other of which is just a delightful piece of news."

"We could do with some 'delightful'," said Ron. "Let's start with that."

"That forensics officer, who underneath all those white overalls seems to be a very attractive young woman, going by the name of Sergeant Singleton, spoke of Inspector Copper as her 'husb...' before she caught herself and referred to him by his rank. I think those two are married!"

Ron laughed. "Now that, Mrs Faye, is a very good piece of detective work. Well done. I'd love to know the story behind that. Although," he reflected, "there's nothing in the world to stop a husband and wife working together in the pursuit of the solution to a crime. I can think of one outstanding example. So what was the other piece of news?"

"Now this one is obviously relevant to the case, judging by Sergeant Singleton's reticence and Inspector Copper's swift action in shutting me down."

"And it is ...?"

"That plastic evidence bag which got loaded into the van held a rather grubby pair of the famous gloves which the dig team have to wear. Why they're of interest, and where they came from, I have no idea."

"Then, love, I suggest we head up to the barrow and see if we can glean anything about what the police have been up to there," said Ron.

"Off we go then," replied Tania, linking her arm with her husband's as the couple made for the farmyard's exit gate.

*

On arrival at the excavation site, the pair found members of the dig team standing in a loose group gazing disconsolately at the spoil heap, whose soil showed signs of having been vigorously turned over. And despite Edward Wilton's determined exhortation of 'Right, everybody. We've got a job to do, so let's get back to work', there was a marked reluctance to move, as everybody lingered for several moments, with many sideways glances aimed at one another. Eventually, however, the group dispersed in various directions.

"Let's have a word with Anne Langford," suggested Tania, as she watched the mature student disappearing into the tent at the side of the barrow, while Victoria Whaddon vanished back down the path to the farm, Stephen Tisbury made his way over to the spoil heap and half-heartedly picked up a sieve, and George Cheverell followed the team leader into the interior of the barrow. "She's probably the one most likely to give us a direct answer."

"We'll give it a go," agreed Ron, and the two started towards the tent, only to be virtually pushed aside by a breathless George.

"Sorry," he apologised. "Almost forgot the shoe covers. Edward's not happy. He's sure the police have been in there messing things up." He dived into the tent, emerging seconds later with a handful of the blue plastic items and hurrying back towards the barrow.

Tania pushed aside the entrance flap of the tent.

"Oh for goodness sake, what is it now, George?" was the barked greeting, before Anne realised the identity of her visitors. "Sorry about that," she said in considerably more subdued tones. "You'll have to excuse me. I think we're all on edge today. This new visit by the police has unsettled everyone. And look at the mess they've left in here." She gestured to the items on the table. "Everything jumbled about, after I try to keep it all neat and orderly. I'd be very interested to know if they had a search warrant to justify all this. And always more questions. I think we all just wish the whole thing was over and done with."

"I'm sure we all wish that," said Tania. "Not least Leah. This is not the most pleasant thing to be hanging over the farm. But you say the inspector was asking questions again?"

"That's right."

"What sort of questions?" enquired Ron.

"Mostly about the equipment," said Anne, beginning to sort the collection of gloves, shoe covers and excavation trowels into neat piles and containers. "Who uses what, who has access to this place, that sort of thing. And of course, the answer is everybody. And it's not as if any of it is special in any way. We brought the gloves and shoe covers from a storeroom back at the archaeology department at Camford, and the stainless steel trowels were ordered from a specialist company and arrived on site the first morning." She gave a grim smile. "And my washing-up bowl and toothbrush came from a supermarket in Westchester. So if they were looking for a murder weapon among this lot, all I can say is, good luck."

"Except that I gather from something that the police let drop," said Tania tentatively, unwilling to admit to having viewed the murder scene, "that they have an idea that a sharp item such as one of these trowels might have been used."

"Well, it's not one of mine," retorted Anne robustly. "They came in a box of a dozen, and they all come back to me at the end of each day to be cleaned. And I was missing one for a while, but then it was returned to me by the police. Apparently it had been found in the barrow next to Professor Sutherland's body, but they had ruled it out as having been used in the murder. More than that, I can't tell you."

"I wonder, would Victoria have any equipment of her own that isn't kept up here?" asked Ron.

Anne shrugged. "I have no idea. You'd have to ask her.."

At this moment, George Cheverell appeared in the opening of the tent. "Sorry to disturb you, Anne ..."

"Now what is it, George?" was Anne's impatient response.

"Professor Wilton wants a couple of trowels. We may be about to lift the skull."

"Take them" Anne handed them over with an irritated snort, and George scuttled away. "And now, if you two have finished your own interrogation, I wouldn't mind getting on. It sounds as if I may soon have actual work to do."

"Of course," soothed Tania. "We'll get out of your hair." She and Ron backed out of the tent.

"Not sure what we've learnt from that," remarked

Ron.

"Maybe one or two things," responded Tania absently. Her gaze focussed on the spoil heap, where Stephen could be seen gazing at the disturbed earth with a puzzled frown. "Let's have a word with Stephen."

As the couple approached the young man, he looked up with a wan smile. "I don't know what's been going on," he said. "The police have obviously been searching here for something, but I can't think what. I'm always very careful when I re-examine the excavated soil to make sure we haven't missed anything, but I have a horrible feeling that somebody must think that I haven't been doing my job properly."

"I'm sure you're very diligent," Tania reassured him. "So how exactly does it work?"

"Well, any soil removed during the dig is brought here in buckets," explained Stephen. "Then it's placed on the fine riddle here, and that gets shaken so that all the loose earth drops through and any items remain on the grill. And they're checked to make sure it's not just stones or odd bits of flint. Finds get taken to Anne. Then the loose earth is thrown on the main heap."

"Does the heap get checked to make sure nothing's slipped through?" asked Ron.

"Every so often," said Stephen. "Except that I've never got round to it since ... you know, finding Professor Sutherland and everything."

"So something could be placed in the sieved soil and not be noticed?" said Tania.

"I suppose so," admitted Stephen. "Why?"

"Oh, just a random thought," replied Tania with an air of unconcern. "Anyway, thank you for the explanation. We'll leave you to get on."

At this point, their attention was distracted by the appearance of Edward Wilton at the entrance of the barrow. "Stephen!" he bellowed. "Here! Now!" He withdrew into the darkness.

"I suppose they want help with the skull," said Stephen. "The professor told us he wanted to lift it. He says it's disarticulated, for some reason. Goodness knows why. I'd better go." He darted into the tent and then trotted over towards the barrow, shoe covers and gloves in hand.

Tania took Ron's arm and led him away. "So that business with the spoil heap is what the police were about," she hissed excitely. "That's where they found those gloves that were attracting the forensic people's attention."

"But why?" wondered Ron. "We know that the trowel found next to the dead man wasn't anything to do with the murder. And surely the point of wearing gloves is to avoid leaving fingerprints on a murder weapon. Except that we don't have one."

"There's an answer here somewhere," insisted Tania. "It just needs to be uncovered."

"Well then," said Ron, "you'd better use your fine analytical librarian's brain to puzzle it out. Do you suppose a cup of tea would help?"

"It certainly wouldn't hurt," smiled Tania.

"And a choccy biccie?"

A chuckle. "Now you're talking."

"Then let's head back to the farm, and I'll get the kettle on."

*

The tea and biscuits having been satisfactorily consumed, Ron took the cups back out to the kitchen to wash up. A few minutes later, he returned to ask, "Shall I get on with sorting something out for lunch?", only to receive no reply, as Tania sat gazing unfocussed at the wall, evidently deep in thought. Ron withdrew silently into the kitchen and softly closed the door.

An hour later he returned, to find Tania pacing up and down murmuring to herself.

"What's that, love?" he enquired.

"Disarticulated," came the unexpected reply.

"That's what Stephen said about the skull from the main chamber, wasn't it?" said Ron. "Seems a bit odd. I mean, they can't have been expecting the skeleton to be exactly chatty, can they? Not having been dead for x-amount of years."

"Nit!" retorted Tania with a smile. "Disarticulated – not inarticulate."

"The difference being …?

"Don't you remember that programme we saw on TV a while back about people excavating dinosaur skeletons in the American desert? At one point they discovered the tail of an animal whose bones were still connected, just as they were when the creature died. In other words, articulated. But the new skull sounds as if it was out of position. So why?" She drew a breath. "I need to talk to Victoria," she announced with sudden resolution.

"Fine. There's a casserole in, but it won't come to any harm. Let me turn the oven down, and I'll come with you."

Th couple found Victoria in the hay-barn, crouched as she pored over the newly-arrived skull from the excavation. "Any thoughts about your new friend?" asked Tania.

Victoria looked up. "Not as yet. But I'm looking forward to making his acquaintance," she replied.

"Do you think he could be Beowulf's father?" enquired Ron.

"Maybe." A shy smile.

"I gather, according to something Stephen said, that the skull was disarticulated from the body," said Tania. "Can we tell why? Could the man have been beheaded?"

"Oh no," said Victoria. "There's no evidence of that. I can't see any sign of damage to the skull itself, nor I'm told to the cervical vertebrae."

"But yet it was removed from its original position. Why would that be? And when?"

Victoria gave a helpless shrug. "I can't tell you. It could have been in antiquity."

"Or more recently?

A shake of the head. "I honestly couldn't say."

"Let's leave Victoria to concentrate on her work, love," suggested Ron. "I think that's about all we can learn at present. So let's go and have some lunch, and you can give it some thought later." The couple left the barn, with Tania casting lingering backward looks as they went.

Chapter 19

After lunch, a companionable enough but not particularly conversational meal, Ron cleared away the plates and then returned to the sitting room to find Tania still buried in thought.

"Still figuring it all out, love?" he enquired, and receiving an absent-minded nod in reply, continued, "I'm off for the obligatory siesta. Join me?"

Tania, seemingly far away, came back and focussed her attention on him. "Sorry, darling. I've not been exactly the life and soul over lunch, have I? Still thinking, I'm afraid. Give me a few minutes, and I'll be with you."

"Deal." Ron retired to the bedroom, stretched out on the bed, and was soon fast asleep. When he awoke, it was to find that he was still alone. He made his way through to the kitchen, to find Tania seated at the table with the pieces of a jigsaw puzzle spread out in front of her. "Where did that come from, love?" he asked.

"At the back of the hall cupboard," replied Tania. "I only came across the box by accident. I went to get my coat, because my brain was buzzing and I thought I'd just get some fresh air for five minutes before coming to lie down. But when I put my head through the bedroom door, you were lying there, gone to the world, snuffling away with an angelic expression on your face, and I thought it would be a shame to disturb you. And then it occurred to me that jigsaw puzzles are very good for the brain. They promote logical thinking, and make you see things in a different way from what appears normal."

Ron looked over his wife's shoulder. "You mean that the bit you thought was a wheel on a locomotive turns out to be part of the cat."

Tania smiled. "Something like that."

"And is it working?"

"Perhaps. One or two pieces are slowly falling

into place."

Ron surveyed the table. "It looks as if you've still got a long way to go."

"All the best puzzles are difficult," replied Tania. "But I'll get there."

"So can I help? Or would it be better if I leave you to it and just plonk myself in front of the television for the evening?"

"You could always saunter down to the Drover's Rest later if you like," suggested Tania.

"On my own?" Ron sounded as if he was no great fan of the idea. "I'd rather we go together."

"Afraid of the big bad murderer stalking the lanes of Upson Parva?" grinned Tania. "Let me get on with my mental exercises, and we'll see."

Ron reluctantly settled down to watch television, whose offerings consisted of far too many news programmes, trips through the universe in a variety of spacecraft involving numerous unpleasant alien races, and a murder mystery which was satisfactorily solved in short order by a resourceful ecclesiastic. During one advertising break he ventured into the kitchen with a suggestion of "A bite of supper, love?", to be rewarded by a vague "Mmm. Lovely." And after placing a plate of sandwiches and a glass of wine at Tania's elbow, acknowledged by a brief kiss and a soft "Thank you, darling" as her eyes scarcely left the jigsaw puzzle before her, he accepted defeat and returned to his solitary viewing.

But after a while, he was brought to his feet by a sudden explosive "Yes!" from the direction of the kitchen, with Tania appearing in the doorway, eyes shining in triumph.

"Got it, love?" enquired Ron breathlessly.

"I do believe I have," replied Tania with a beaming smile, which then faded swiftly into uncertainty. "That is, I think I have. Because it's the only way that everything we've been told fits."

"And are you going to tell me?"

Tania's reluctance was plain. "But what if I'm wrong?"

"You never are, love," said Ron confidently.

"But if this isn't the way it happened and we have to go on trying to find out the truth, it's going to be very difficult to look everybody in the eye without them clamming up completely, or else thinking I'm an utter fool."

"Never that," declared Ron stoutly. "But don't you think you ought to at least tell Leah. You know, remove the sword of Damocles that's hanging over the whole place? I know she'd be glad of that."

"She'd have to call the police," objected Tania. "And I'm not sure that they'd be too enthusiastic at this hour. I'd rather leave it to the morning."

"In that case," said Ron with determination, looking at his watch, "let's adjourn to the Drover's for a drink to take our minds off the subject."

"Sorry, but I'm not sure that's a good idea," said Tania. "You never know who we might run into there."

With a sigh, Ron decided to surrender. "In that case, love, come and sit down. We can finish off that bottle of wine, and I have a suspicion that there's another one still on the rack. We'll watch something mind-numbing on TV to take our minds off everything, and then have an early night. How's that for a plan?"

"Mr. Faye, you are a wonderfully understanding man," smiled Tania, closing in for a hug.

"As I believe I may have mentioned before, I have my uses," replied Ron with a grin. "Now, let me grab a glass."

*

"Good morning, you two," said Leah as she answered the door of the farmhouse. "This is a bit early. I don't think anyone's about yet."

"That's actually the point," replied Tania. "We've got some news for you – well, everybody, really – and we didn't want to wait until everyone had dispersed about the place. I don't think it'll keep."

Leah looked closely at the solemn expression on Tania's features. "Are you telling me what I think you're telling me?" she asked. "Have you worked out what happened?"

"I think I have," said Tania. "Whether it's good enough for the police I don't know, but in my mind it's the only way things fit together. So I thought, for everyone's peace of mind, I ought to explain my thinking."

Leah stepped back. "Well, come in, come in. You can tell me everything, and then we can decide what to do."

"On the whole," intervened Ron, "I think it might be better if we got everyone together and told them in one go. Less chance of anyone relating duff information to anyone else." He gave a half-smile. "And bearing in mind that even I don't know what Tania's figured out. I'm as much in the dark as you."

At that moment, Edward Wilton emerged from Henge Cottage, with Stephen Tisbury at his heels. Seeing him, Leah called to him.

"Professor Wilton, can I have a word?" She dropped her voice as the archaeologist approached. "Mrs Faye has some news which she would like your whole party to hear. I wonder if it would be possible to gather them all together. Perhaps in the hay-barn."

"What's all this about, Mrs Faye?" Edward sounded puzzled.

"Tania will be happy to tell you in just a moment," said Ron firmly. "And I think Leah's suggestion is a very good one. And Leah, I expect you'd like Mary to join the group. I'm sure she ought to be aware of what's going on."

"I'll call her," said Leah, heading for The Piggery, just as George Cheverell, Henry Gifford and Jane Sherrington arrived chatting at the entrance to the farmyard, having evidently walked up from the village together. And as Edward knocked at the door of Tumulus Cottage to summon Victoria Whaddon and Anne Langford, Leah made her way over to the group of new arrivals to acquaint them with the proposed arrangements.

"Ready for this, love?" asked Ron, as the last person disappeared into the hay-barn.

"As ready as I'll ever be," responded Tania shakily. "So much guesswork, and so little physical evidence. But heigh ho, let's give it a try." She entered the barn, to find the company seated around on chairs, upturned buckets, and bales of straw. They turned their eyes towards her expectantly as she stood silhouetted in the doorway.

"As I'm sure you must all realise," she began, "I need to talk about Professor Malcolm Sutherland."

"Must you?" sighed Anne Langford. "Haven't we thought enough about him over the last few days? It would be nice to have a chance to think about something else."

"And I promise you that that's what I want too," said Tania. "But while his unsolved murder is hanging over us all, that is a luxury none of us can enjoy."

"It's fine for you," remarked Mary Winterbourne. "You were never on the receiving end of his behaviour."

"And that's what I want to talk about," replied Tania. "Because all of you were. To a greater or lesser extent."

"Not me," spoke up Jane Sherrington. "He scarcely spoke to me from the time he arrived. Not that I'm complaining. Because I witnessed the way he spoke to some other people. But I was lucky. I stayed out of his firing line. And so did my Henry here, didn't you, darling?" Alongside her, Henry gave a nod and a muted grunt of agreement.

"Sorry if I didn't make myself clear," said Tania. "We all know that you two couldn't have had anything to do with Malcolm's death. And the same applies to Leah. She was many miles away."

"But that's not to say that I didn't know what kind of man he was," stated Leah. "But for me, thank goodness, it was all a very long time ago."

"Whereas," continued Tania, "the same can't be said for the rest of you. To a greater or lesser extent, he made himself unpleasant to everyone here." She turned to the farm manager. "Including you, Mary. Although I doubt if he truly understood that his advances to you were as obnoxious as you found them. A pest of that kind is not necessarily easy to deter. Some might think that the only way to remove the problem was to remove the pest. In extreme fashion.

"Then we come to the members of the dig team. Not all from the University of Camford, although most of you are. So what motives might each of you have to wish Malcolm Sutherland out of the way? One common motive might be jealousy. Professor Wilton, you were understandably put out when Malcolm was brought in to head up the archaeological investigation over and above you. The insult to your status must have been huge. And when this was coupled with the remarks Malcolm was heard to make about your overall competence and suitability for your job, either here or back at the university, does it take a particularly great stretch of the imagination to contemplate how your rage might have built up until it boiled over into drastic action?

"Then there is action in response to a threat. Who was threatened? Well, for a start, the two younger students, although the threats were of a different nature. Victoria, your abilities were questioned very vocally, and there was a direct threat by Malcolm to ensure that your academic qualifications were put in jeopardy. Did he have the influence to ensure this? I can't tell. But you couldn't be certain that all your hard work wouldn't have been for nothing. And Stephen, you received a threat of a different kind. Two kinds, in fact. Firstly, there was the approach by Malcolm, as witnessed by the landlord of the local pub, of a similar kind to that experienced by Mary."

Stephen blushed furiously, and many of the group reacted with horrified puzzlement as the import of Tania's words dawned on them.

"And because this approach was also rejected," continued Tania, "the professor was heard to utter threats of a similar kind to those received by Victoria. Academic ruin. And of course, speaking of Victoria, you might have had a secondary motive, that of wishing to protect an object of your affections. It's no secret, however much you might wish it to be, that you have, to put it mildly, a soft spot for Victoria. Seeing her under threat, might you take it upon yourself to rescue her from her position by the use of extreme means?

"And then, of course, there's the question of Malcolm's gratuitous unpleasantness to the two remaining members of the dig team, George Cheverell and Anne Langford. George is the only member of that team not to hail from the university, being the local man. And a very well-thought-of local man, if what Billy Charlton from the Drover's Rest says is true. 'Our local history buff', he called him. 'You want to know anything, just ask George'. Unfortunately, Professor Sutherland did not share that opinion. He called him a yokel, and publicly demeaned him. And this was after George had attempted to impress him with his own little museum of historical finds. No, Malcolm had no time for George. He brushed him off repeatedly. And he behaved the same way towards Anne. Spoke of her age in highly unflattering terms, and sneered at the contribution she made to the team's work. Not ..." A quiet smile. "Not that

Anne is the type to take such behaviour too much to heart, if my conversations with her are to be believed. She was extremely forthright in her opinions of Malcolm Sutherland, and wasn't hesitant in expressing them to me. Unlike, I may say, the majority of you." Tania looked around the people assembled. "Most of you evaded my enquiries at the start. You were unwilling to express any adverse opinion of your former leader. Thank goodness for the other people I managed to speak to, who gave a truer picture of the situation."

"I can see where you're coming from, Tania dear," intervened Leah, "but not where you're going. We all became aware that Malcolm was not what you'd call a nice man. Lord knows, I had better cause to know that than these others, who'd only known him a matter of days. But you don't explain how any of this led to what happened last Saturday night."

"You're right, Leah," conceded Tania. "Was anything I've said a good and sufficient motive for murder? Perhaps not. So now we come on to the actual night of Malcolm's death. One inhibiting factor was the fact that everybody appeared to have a solid alibi, although when these were examined in a little more detail, none were as solid as they seemed. And there was one factor that caught my eye - the behaviour of Malcolm himself on that evening. There were incongruous elements. He appeared to be excited or tense, for some reason. So I've been told by more than one person. He bought a round of drinks in the pub. Unheard of. There seemed to be an undefinable air of urgency about him - he brusquely brushed aside offers of help on the following morning. And then, unaccountably, he appeared in the darkened farmyard at midnight. This was evidently him on his way up to the dig site. But why? Could the reason for all this be that he believed himself to be on the verge of a discovery, one so significant that he had no intention of allowing anyone else a share in the kudos. And what might that have been? You were in the process of penetrating the final burial chamber of the barrow, but there was an odd factor. There was disturbance to the soil and stones of the entrance. Had someone been there beforehand? In antiquity, it was suggested. A tomb robber hunting for valuables? Such things are not restricted to modern adventure films - witness all the royal tombs of Egypt, with one notable exception.

"So had Malcolm guessed that such an incursion had occurred? Possibly. Had he even glimpsed some tiny glint of something which led to him unceremoniously hauling everyone else away from the site and ending work for the day? I'm guessing. And what might such an object be? We have hints. There was a bronze torc discovered earlier, belonging to the presumed young warrior in the first chamber. It was fair to assume that the main chamber contained the body of someone of far higher status - a chieftain, a war leader, perhaps. And if he were buried with his own torc, how magnificent might that be? Not mere bronze, surely. And torcs of that type were designed never to be removed. But it was found that the skull of the chieftain was disarticulated from the rest of the skeleton. In other words, the head was removed from the body. And what would be a better reason to carry out such sacrilege than to lay hands on the chieftain's torc? Tomb robbers are not known for their niceties. But perhaps the robber was discovered in mid-attempt. Perhaps he fled, or received extreme punishment from the guardians of the barrow. And perhaps, in the midst of this, the torc was let fall and remained in the rubble of the tomb."

"This is all fascinating speculation, Mrs Faye," broke in Edward Wilton, "but it brings us no nearer to identifying the person responsible for killing Professor Sutherland."

"And I apologise if I'm being long-winded," said

Tania, "but I felt it necessary to set the scene. One in which Malcolm Sutherland could well have been on the verge of a breath-taking discovery. But was I alone in putting these thoughts together? I suspect not. Someone else must have been of the same opinion. And that someone was the person who appeared in the farmyard only moments after Malcolm had left for the dig site, the person with a torch which accounts for the flickering light witnessed by Stephen Tisbury. That person perhaps caught sight of Malcolm as he left, and immediately understood his intention. They followed him to the site, and must have caught him in the moment of discovery.

"Now it's improbable that that person could have been Stephen. He would never have volunteered the information he did. And if it had been Professor Wilton, surely Stephen would have heard him leave the cottage in that moment. It's equally unlikely that Mary Winterbourne would have been the person who followed in Malcolm's footsteps – what interest would she have in strange goings-on up at the dig at midnight? And although Victoria Whaddon and Anne Langford cannot provide a definitive alibi for each other, isn't it implausible that either could have left their cottage, committed the crime, and returned completely undetected by the other?

"But there remains one person whose location cannot be verified. One person whose whole life so far has been devoted to the uncovering of historical objects. One person whose self-confessed longing for gold could have brought them to the barrow in the dead of that fateful night. George Cheverell."

Chapter 20

"You're mad!" George leapt to his feet and regarded Tania with blazing eyes. "This is the most ridiculous story I've ever heard. You've made it all up."

Tania shook her head. There was an expression of sorrow and regret in her eyes. "And in a way, I have. I can't show you any actual evidence. But I can't see how, putting together all the little wisps of information I've gathered since I arrived here, it could have been any other way."

She looked at the company gathered around the room, each with an expression of varying bewilderment and disbelief. "I've already told you why I've come to the conclusion I have on the question of opportunity. That's one of the things I believe the police consider when they're looking into a crime – opportunity, means, and motive. And George's alibi was the most obvious, because he had left the group to return to his own cottage long before you all reached the farm. But it was also the one with the most obvious flaw, because there was nobody to verify it. And the significance is that that pause gave George the opportunity to put together in his mind the straws in the wind from the previous few hours. He had been withdrawn abruptly from his work on the dig at Professor Sutherland's orders. Why so sudden? The work for the day had been swiftly brought to a halt immediately afterwards. For what reason? Then there was the unaccountable bonhomie which the professor displayed that evening down at the pub. Most out of character. Also his air of excitement, not well concealed, noted by more than one person. And his adamant refusal to accept any further offer of assistance from George as the party left the Drover's Rest. I believe George drew the same conclusion which I have - namely, that Professor Sutherland had some inkling of an imminent wonderful discovery, and he wanted to keep it for himself. So perhaps George's intention when he set out from home that night was simply to forestall the professor by examining the dig for himself. Here was his opportunity.

"But what he found, when he reached the farm, was Professor Sutherland on his way to the barrow. He followed the professor through the fields, but the alpacas knew George as a friend, so made no fuss. He then found him in the process of uncovering by torchlight the item which both suspected was there. I imagine that the professor was so concentrated by his find that he was unaware of George's presence behind him. But George could clearly see what had been found, and in that moment he realised that perhaps the greatest coup of his own archaeological career was about to be stolen from him. Was it rage? Was it jealousy? I can't see into his mind. But what I can visualise was what was in his hand – his old faithful trowel which had brought him so many finds over the years. A trowel similar to all the others on the site – wide-bladed, pointed, and with an edge like a knife. And suddenly, that trowel blade was buried in Malcolm Sutherland's back, probably killing him instantly. So there you have the means - the murder weapon.

"Now there must have been some amount of blood issuing from the wound, but that was where George's long-ingrained discipline as an archaeologist came to his aid. Because I believe he had put on a pair of the protective gloves stored in the site tent before entering the barrow. Gloves which prevented any blood getting on his hands, and which also had the secondary benefit of avoiding the leaving of fingerprints on the murder weapon – not that that would have been an issue. Why shouldn't George's fingerprints be on his own trowel? It would be odd if they weren't. So the gloves in question were discarded and concealed in the spoil heap as George left the site, only to be retrieved later by the police forensics team. I wondered why they would be of interest to them, when the trowel lying at Malcolm Sutherland's side was proved not to be involved in the crime. There had to be another reason.

"And then there arose the question of motive. One obvious one would have been the persistent demeaning or insulting behaviour of Professor Sutherland towards George. But then, which of you all hadn't been on the receiving end of something similar?" Tania looked around the faces all regarding her with rapt concentration. "So there had to be more. And so I returned to the question of the mysterious find. What could it be? There were clues. A bronze torc had already been discovered amid the remains of the so-called young warrior. The main occupant of the barrow surely warranted greater honours. And when I learnt that the man's skull had been found disarticulated – that is to say, not connected – from the neck vertebrae, the conclusion seemed obvious. It had already been suggested that the burial had been disturbed long ago by a presumed tomb robber, but yet here was a great treasure still in the tomb, if not in its original position. Had that robber been disturbed, and let fall his prize? Probably. And in my conversations with George, he had not been able to conceal his yearning for gold - the ultimate treasure. So what other conclusion was I to draw than that here we had an astonishingly precious item - a gold torc, designed never to be removed from the neck of the chieftain in life and which remained with him in death, only to be sacrilegiously stolen from his body by the displacing of his head. So there was the torc for the taking - a fabulous addition to George's little personal museum, but one which could never ever be revealed to anyone. And so, clutching his new-found treasure, George vanished into the night."

The whole group turned to look in George's direction, shock visible on everyone's features. He stood and looked around at each of them, before focussing his attention back on Tania. "That, Mrs Faye," he said, with a tight smile, "was quite the *tour de force*. You must be exhausted after the effort of creating such a formidable work of fiction. Because that's all it is. A complete fairy tale. Since, as you so helpfully pointed out to us all, you haven't a single shred of concrete evidence." But suddenly his eyes grew wide and the smile faded.

"She may well not," came the unexpected voice of Inspector Copper, who had appeared silently at Tania's shoulder. She whirled, to find the inspector, attended by his sergeant, standing behind her with an expression of quiet satisfaction on his face. "Unfortunately for you, Mr Cheverell, we do."

A babble of voices suddenly broke out, including an unbelieving 'But how...?' from George, before the inspector succeeded in quieting everyone with a commanding gesture.

"And although I confess it pains me to say it, I must admit that I believe Mrs Faye was remarkably accurate in her summary of the situation." Copper gave Tania the tiniest bow of acknowledgement, in which she thought she could detect a grudging hint of humour. "But there are things she could not know. For example, our forensics people discovered a tiny splinter of wood on the back of the clothing which Malcolm Sutherland was wearing at the time of his death. Unaccountable. We too came to the conclusion that an archaeological trowel was the murder weapon, but all the trowels on the site were of solid steel. But then I recalled something. Mr Cheverell, you were very unwise to invite me in to view your display of finds as I was passing your cottage the other day. Because among them was your own trowel, which I recalled had a wooden handle in a very poor state of repair. And I came to believe that a comparison of the splinter and that handle will reveal that they are of identical material."

"But you can't ..." protested George, before his

voice faded into silence.

Copper smiled. "I have a search warrant that says I can, Mr Cheverell," he replied. "Just as I suspect, in view of Mrs Faye's deductions in the matter ..." Another nod of acknowledgement. "... that there is an item of considerable historic significance to be found somewhere on your premises. We shall see. But what is not in doubt is the fact that a pair of gloves recovered from the dig site spoil heap, imperfectly cleaned by rubbing them in soil, still retain minute remnants of Professor Sutherland's blood. And what gives them the greatest significance is the confirmation by my forensic colleagues, having just completed tests at remarkable speed, that the interior of these gloves has unmistakeable traces of DNA. Your DNA, Mr Cheverell. And nobody else's."

There was a long pause as George slowly subsided into his seat. "It's the most beautiful thing I've ever seen," he said, almost to himself. He looked up at Tania. "You're very clever, Mrs Faye. You were right. It is a torc. A thick rope of twisted wires with dragon-head terminals, all in pure gold. The workmanship ..." He gazed unfocussed into the distance, his voice fading, before resuming. "You'll find it on my bookshelves, inspector. I hollowed out a book on Anglo-Saxon history as a hiding place. Appropriate, don't you think?" A wan smile. "I couldn't help myself. I had to have it ..." His voice broke, and he subsided in sobs.

Copper turned to his colleague. "Sergeant Radley, if you would be so good as to take Mr Cheverell into custody."

"This way, sir, if you please." Radley crossed to George and placed a hand on his shoulder, and the stunned-looking amateur archaeologist followed the sergeant out into the farmyard, where Radley could be faintly heard reciting, "George Cheverell, I am placing you under arrest on suspicion of the murder of Malcolm

Sutherland. You do not have to say anything, ..." The voices faded beneath a rising murmur of speculation from the barn's occupants.

*

"I don't know how to thank you," said Leah for the fourth time, topping up the couple's whisky glasses as the three sat in the farmhouse living room.

Tania gave a slightly embarrassed shrug. "What else are friends for?"

"And I'm still baffled as to how you put all that together."

"I think Tania is something of a follower of Sherlock Holmes in that respect," smiled Ron, with a fond gaze in his wife's direction. "In other words, she eliminates the impossibilities, and then whatever remains, however improbable, must be the truth."

"It'll rattle the village," observed Leah. "Whatever George may have done, and goodness knows there's no excuse for it, he's very popular. Some people will find it hard to credit the truth."

"Then it's a relief, if I can put it that way, that he's admitted what happened," remarked Tania. "But I agree. I liked George. Very much. But it just goes to show what some people will do when there's too much temptation laid out in front of them."

"And the Lord preserve the rest of us from that," intoned Leah, downing her drink.

"Amen to that," said Ron, following suit. "And now, if you don't mind, I think Tania and I will fade away as unobtrusively as possible. She's had quite enough limelight for one day, and if she's anything like me, she'll be glad to sleep in her own bed tonight."

"I can't blame you," smiled Leah. "And as for fading away, that shouldn't be too much of a problem. All the others were disappearing in various directions as we came in here. That inspector of yours was just about to drive off with George in the back of his car, sergeant alongside him, and Mary was about to vanish into her office with a long list of phone calls to make. She's determined to contact all our clients and make sure that everyone knows that we're completely blameless in all of this murder kerfuffle. Henry said he was going to go round, arm in arm with Jane, and talk to all the animals to tell them the news - he says alpacas are very intuitive - and then do the same in the village later. I think they're both glad that a cloud's been lifted. And I heard Professor Wilton gather together his team with determined words about keeping calm and carrying on, before shepherding them off towards the barrow. Except for Victoria, that is. She's gone back to work in her barn."

"Actually," said Tania, "I'm glad. I'd like a word with her before we go."

"Why don't you do that, love," suggested Ron, "while I go and chuck our stuff together and get it in the car. Shouldn't take me more than a few minutes."

Tania leant across and kissed her husband. "You do look after me."

"I keep telling you I have my uses," grinned Ron. "Now off you go. I'll see you in a bit."

When Tania entered the hay-barn, it was to find Victoria leaning over the newly-delivered skull of the chieftain and gazing intently into its empty eye-sockets. At Tania's arrival, she straightened up with a faintly embarrassed air.

"You'll be glad to get back to your normal work," remarked Tania, affecting not to notice the other's discomfiture.

"Actually, I think it's going to be better than normal," replied Victoria, her eyes beginning to shine.

"How so?"

"Professor Wilton has proposed that I should write a paper on the whole excavation - well, all the scientific parts, anyway - and submit it as a major part of my Masters. He says he can think of no better way to demonstrate my ability. And he's going to pull every string he can think of to establish our own museum at Camford, instead of everything going to the County Museum at Westchester. And he wants me to produce a guide book. He says the university authorities owe him a favour. He's going to call it 'The Upson Downs Barrow Project', and it's going to feature our chieftain as the star exhibit."

"That sounds wonderful," enthused Tania. "Congratulations. And your chieftain here – any thoughts as to a name?" She waited with raised eyebrows.

Victoria smiled shyly. "I'm going to call him Hrothgar. It's the name of a famous Norse warrior hero king. And he appears in the ancient Anglo-Saxon poem 'Beowulf'. So ..."

"Very suitable," smiled Tania. "I just wanted to say goodbye and wish you luck. And now I'll leave you two alone together," she twinkled.

Victoria blushed. "Goodbye. And thank you - from all of us."

When Tania re-entered the farmyard, she found Ron standing alongside the car, giving Leah a farewell kiss. "And don't think we shan't be expecting starring rôles in the next production you direct for R.O.A.D.S.," he said with a grin.

"Guaranteed, dearie," responded Leah. "Now be off with you. I have a farm to run."

Ron held the car door for his wife, before going round to climb in at the driver's door. He started the engine. "Anywhere in particular, love?" he enquired facetiously.

"Home," said Tania in heartfelt tones. "And if anyone should phone or come knocking at the door ... don't answer!"

Ron let in the clutch and, with a farewell wave from the couple, the car pulled out of the farmyard and started down the dusty lane towards Upson Parva.

*   *   *

The Copper & Co Murder Mysteries

Murderer's Honeymoon
Even on an idyllic tropical island, murder never takes a holiday

Murder At Witch's Holt
Dark secrets lead to a strange death at a spooky manor house

Buccaneer's Murder
A wealthy businessman lies dead aboard his luxury private yacht

The Ramston Murder Mysteries

Murdered By Moonlight
Dramatic death at a Cornish open-air theatre

Manuscript For Murder
An ancient abbey with an all-too-modern corpse

The Whodunnit Murder
A fun murder game turns serious when a real body appears

*   *   *

Printed in Great Britain
by Amazon

55595954R00116